Education is hall mark of our Social character

Dedicated
To my mother, **Sukhbiri**,
a great story teller

About Author

The author, Bir Singh Yadav, was born in village Dolcha in Baghpat District of Uttar Pradesh. He did his primary education at his native village and secondary education from Meerut. He completed his Bachelor' degree in Veterinary Science and Animal Husbandry (B.V.Sc. & A.H) in 1979 from Mathura, and Master's degree (M.V.Sc) in the subject of Veterinary Pathology from same place in year 1981. Apart from publishing 7 Research Papers from his Master's degree, he has authored 2 books for general readership in digital format.

Author has had a variegated, multidisciplinary carrier. This includes, as Veterinary Officer in large animal treatment as well as in the poultry industry. As a General Manager at a Breeder Poultry Farm. As a private practitioner and consultant vet. As a School Principal. As an LIC agent. And a freelance writer in Hindi and English language. For 4 years he has also dabbled as senior reporter in a Hindi newspaper. He also served as teaching faculty and as a Deputy Registrar in a Private University.

Presently he is based as Meerut and working as content writer, translator, and Insurance adviser. A keen runner since his school days, the author runs cross country and half marathon races. He loves outing, and adventure sports.

PREFACE

We are, forever searching for something in our lives. And tragedy begins when we actually find it. Yet search is integral to life and it can culminate both in joy as well as intrigue. Risk has to be taken and life has to be accepted as it unfolds, whether it is to our liking or not.

Dev realized as a School boy that mainstream medicine was a farce. He studied medicine and became a Veterinary Doctor. Torn between precept and practice, he realized that farce is far more ubiquitous phenomenon in society than he had ever imagined. It is like all running in a direction simply because others were running in that direction, without knowing where to.

There is an Urdu couplet which says: I had taken just one step in the direction my heart indicated, and for the rest of my life, my destiny searched hard for me. Do we reach our desired destination in our lifetime? Or we end up calling whatever we get, or reach to, as our destination, or destiny?

Is education limited to getting diplomas and degrees irrespective of their relevance to evolving society? And that too by all means, fair or foul? Perhaps yes. This explains why cheating in examination is so rampant. That's why we have a market for fake degrees.

When most things around us are fake, an occasional genuine is seen as threat. There was a community of the born-blind, so goes a story. A man with good eyesight walks into this community. He empathizes with community and wants to do something for it. But the community gangs up against him, declares his activities suspicious, calls him `blind'! The man gets a wind of it and runs away to save his life. Same is the case with Dev, the protagonist of this story, except that he doesn't run away. He stays put.

My sincere thanks to my daughter Eisha, son-in-law Ankit Aggarwal and their daughter Ahana. They were an excellent host for 6 months of my stay in South Africa, where this book was written. Thanks are also due to my niece Zenia and Jasmine, my friends Dr.Vivek Ranjan Chaurasia, Vineet Gupta, my brothers Keshav and Birender, and sister

Rajeshwari.

-   Author

1

They were on friendly term after a long disconnect.

Dr. Dev Purohit and Dr. Mukesh Prajapati spoke to each other on their cell phones daily. Prajapati was in the process of selecting a suitable match for his daughter, Vinita, a school teacher. Dev was doing the background check of a boy – Vikas Verma, who was shortlisted as a prospective groom.

Based on his verification, Dr. Dev reported that the boy wasn't suitable for Vinita and suggested that they look for a different match. Dr. Mukesh Prajapati felt the boy was perfect. Could Dev give reasons for his unfavorable opinion?

"Boy is eccentric and a loner. Doesn't socialize much. He suffered nervous breakdown during his Post Graduation. His father Col. K. K. Verma is a social misfit. No one invites him to any social ceremony. He broke away from his brothers and sisters, and even his parents." Dev explained.

"You can't give a diagnosis by picking up one or two symptoms. The boy is a merit scholar. I have talked to his teachers. His father's follies shouldn't be put on him," Mukesh countered.

"It's the question of your daughter's life, Prajapati, and not a chapter in clinical diagnosis. Basic human nature never changes. I suggest you select some other match from your shortlist, or float a fresh matrimonial ad," said Dr.Purohit. He had done a thorough check on the boy, Vikas Verma, working as Asst. Registrar at Ramjilal University, Baghpat, Uttar Pradesh.

Vinita would marry Vikas if all went well.

Dev and Mukesh were batch mates at Mathura Veterinary College, and best friends too. They did their graduation and post-graduation together. Dev found placement in poultry industry, and Mukesh in Dairy. For the 10 years of their service they remained in touch. Then, they lost touch.

Mukesh was searching matrimonial alliance for his daughter. One match was from Meerut. Who else could do a better check on that family than Dev, a domicile of Meerut city? With this objective in mind he searched for Dev's whereabouts and found him.

Dev and his estranged wife, Parul Purohit, had married off their one and only daughter, Veena, 2 years ago. Estrangement with his wife had ruffled Dev hard. Many of his friends, including Prajapati, distanced themselves from him. Who wants to be friendly with a broken home?

Now camaraderie was returning.

Search for a groom injected new life into the fading friendship. Dev and Mukesh, the famed PP (Purohit-Prajapati) duo of college days bonded once again.

2

Marriages are made in heaven. Vinita got married to Vikas Verma, the same guy who the two friends, PP, rated differently. Purohit rejected him and Prajapati, the girl's father, accepted him.

Following marriage, Vinita resigned from her school teacher's job. Vikas, her husband, got her employed in Humanities department of Ramjilal University where he himself worked as Asst. Registrar.

Some unpleasant developments saw Vikas sacked from his job. Vinita continued teaching there and the couple lived in the staff quarters in the University campus. Vikas was sacked for his alleged links to a fake degree racket. A band of policemen descended on campus with mark sheets bearing the logo of Ramjilal University. All these were fake and carried signatures of Vikas Verma. That was shocking for Verma. Someone may have fooled him to sign them. Off and on he had been a Public Relations Officer, Hostel Warden and even Information Officer. Multitasking made him extremely worked up but he stayed put, hoping it would end someday. He was post-graduate in computer engineering and was selected in University to teach computer science. He hoped that multitasking would end someday and he would be able to concentrate on his primary job - teaching Computer Science.

Over the course of his multiple assignments at the university he signed countless documents including student identity cards. His signatures could have been lifted and planted on forged mark sheets. University, however, was in no mood to listen. Vikas was dismissed from service following a report submitted by the Disciplinary Committee. Report accused him of signing forged documents for antisocial elements, who then sold those documents to gullible students.

Vinita already had serious problems adjusting with Vikas, and his parents. Vermas were fussy and meddled in her affairs. Vinita put up with them stoically. Her parents counseled her to be accommodating. Vikas took his parents' side and slighted Vinita, even raised his hand on her on a few occasions.

With Vikas now jobless, Prajapati family was worried all the more for their daughter. Vermas too felt guilty about their son being a financial burden on their daughter-in-law who they had been insulting and harassing for long.

Mukesh regretted ignoring Dev's advice. But it was too late now.

3

"Stand up!" Professor of Gynecology, Dr. H.C. Pant threw a chalk in a corner of the class room. Mukesh was hit. He stood up meekly. There was pin drop silence in class. "Sorry Sir," stammered Mukesh, trying to figure what could have annoyed Dr. Pant. Why was he talking to Dev? Dr. Pant demanded. Mukesh cleared his throat and explained, "Sir we discussed reproductive physiology yesterday when Dev told me that pituitary is the master of endocrine orchestra. Since you said the same thing in the class, I just looked to Dev to acknowledge that he was right." Dr. Pant cooled down and moved on with his discourse.

Dev and Mukesh, the PP – duo, talked long and deep on all issues of life, death and beyond. Post-graduation (PG) hostel was often frequented by parents searching suitable candidates for their daughters. Dev had a brush with 2 proposals which he declined politely. News broke out in hostel and congratulations poured in.

"When is the party?"

"No such thing, why…." laughed Dev.

Reading matrimonial column was popular pass time. Rakesh called out, "this is the match I am responding to." Goverdhan looked into the newspaper and laughed, "Stupid, are you gay, going for same sex marriage? Ad is for bride, not groom!"

Fun was the way in hostel life. Be it boycotting exams or going on a strike for new furniture in the common room.

"Look at the carpet," said Dr. P K Shrivastav, "seems like a handover from the emperor Jahangir." He was lustily cheered and warden was forced to approve new furniture and upholstery for the common room.

Those lucky to get married while studying in college were forced to give 'running commentary' of their first- night.

"How many times did you do it?"

"Well, there can't be a count. Once begun, you go on and on…" said Kunwar Pal (KP).

Dev and Mukesh were going to attend KP's marriage when they were way laid by thugs and stripped of their belongings. PP duo skipped marriage and stayed in police station to register an FIR. Was that foreshadow of KP's tumultuous married life?

Kunwar Pal's wife, in course of time, was diagnosed as full blown case of acute Schizophrenia. In a bout of depression she jumped into a canal along with her 3 children. Passersby rescued her, and her two kids; one kid drowned.

4

Prajapatis arranged a sitting with Vermas. Ailing marriage of Vikas and Vinita was the topic of discussion.

Col. Verma was blunt and unrelenting. Girl must do boy's bidding. Ground reality though was different. Vinita did her best to keep Vikas in good humor, but failed. After several face offs, it transpired that Vikas suffered from bouts of mental depression.

Vinita was married to a professional who turned out to be mentally weak. Her nightmares began right with the seven rounds of the holy fire. As the priest read out homilies for the couple, Col. Verma objected, "Why should the girl's consent be necessary for all that the boy does? Husband is head of the family, not the wife." Vikas was seen grinning from ear to ear. Vinita was upset but occasion demanded restraint.

Patch up meeting ended on a discordant note. Vermas stuck to their line that Vinita was trying to dominate them as well as their son.

Dev, while attending Vinita's marriage, had felt ill at ease. He met the couple - Vinita and Vikas, seated on ceremonial throne, and gave them his blessings. He then sought permission to leave and walked out of the venue. On the way back he got a call.

"Aree yaar, at least you should have taken dinner," it was Mukesh calling.

"Well I gorged on drinks and snacks. Dinner then would have been a mistake. You know how fussy I am about eating. Please relax."

Dev was abstemious eater and iconic health freak right from his school days.

5

Walls have ears, winds can see, nature can predict. This happens in films, in stories, in real life too.

Dev was gifted a piece of cloth for a 3 piece suite in his engagement ceremony. He gave it for tailoring. On delivery, he was shocked. Suite was horribly loose fitted; twice his size. Obviously his measurements got exchanged with another customer. Tailor apologized profusely and purchased another piece of cloth, of Dev's liking, as compensation. Next delivery was a perfect fit. "It is a bad omen. Wedding suite got swapped… what next?" observed a colleague.

Dev didn't believe in luck. He argued over it with a class fellow in school. The classmate believed in preordained destiny, Dev didn't. Don't work hard, don't plan well and then blame destiny for failures, Dev reasoned. The class fellow gave a wry smile, as if to say 'you will learn it the hard way'.

Science doesn't negate supernatural. Sir Isaac Newton defended Astrology. Don't underestimate a science which you haven't studied well, he warned his friend who laughed at Astrology. As life unfolded into rough terrains, Dev remembered the class fellow who believed in destiny and gave him a wry smile. He was right, Dev mused. There is a limit to what labor can yield. In the long last, it's destiny that prevails. Horoscope of Dev's sister did not match with the prospective groom. "They will fight like cats and dogs," said the priest who matched their horoscope. Dev's father, Harichand, a handicapped teacher but a man of modern outlook, went ahead with marriage, regardless. Marriage was short lived. Sister returned to live with her parents. Her husband re-married.

There are higher forces that govern human life, said Bal Gangadhar Tilak at his trial for sedition, "and it may just be that the cause I represent prospers more by my suffering than (my) remaining free."

Do estranged couples suffer a divine diktat? Pitted together by higher forces to promote their respective cause? Was he destined to marry Parul because she was brought up to be a conventional home maker? And he grew up with revolutionary ideas of eating raw food, and living under the open sky, like animals do, i.e. as close to nature as possible? Does it represent some kind of balancing act of destiny?

Nature never plays dice, said Einstein. It shouts aloud what's about to happen. It's we who ignore the elephant in the room, and choose to see only what we want to see.

6

Vinita taught English at Ramjilal University. Her sacked husband stayed with her, hoping for reinstatement. He might have committed a bona fide mistake, he never signed any unauthorized or illegal document, he argued endlessly, but to no effect.

A sacked employee staying in campus was against the decorum of university. But being spouse of a teaching faculty, Vikas had every right to stay with his wife. Could Vinita be sacked, somehow, to see Vikas out of the campus? Idea was mooted by the management. But Vinita was too good a teacher to be sacked on a flimsy ground. She had also filed an FIR against the University for injustice meted to her husband by the University. She could definitely file another FIR to defend her own job. So, the idea to sack Vinita was dropped.

Recording reasons for his dismissal, the University had declared Vikas a patient of Schizophrenia, unfit for university job. Vinita was determined to save her husband's career. If at all her husband needed psychiatric help, she would get him treated. Mental disease, like any other ailment, can be treated and cured. So what if her in-laws weren't cooperative; she will make it on her own. Her father, Mukesh, despised Col. Verma and his wife for being indifferent to his daughter's needs, but could do little to mend their ways. No father can mess with his daughter's marriage. Balraj Sahni played father in 'Neelkamal'. He had a brawl with in-laws of his daughter, and got injured in the ruckus. Seeing him bleed, daughter, Waheeda Rahman, shrieked, "papa blood?!"

"It's not blood my dear," said Sahni, choking, "it is water. Were it blood, wouldn't it boil in rage, and burn this world to ashes seeing you suffer like this?"

Same for Prajapati. Being father, he had to keep a low profile. He reasoned with son-in-law to no end and met anyone and everyone who he felt mattered. Finally, there was a ray of hope. When Vikas was sacked from the University, Col. Verma agreed to put him on intensive psychiatric treatment.

"Have you seen the film, a beautiful mind? Consider your husband as the genius professor of this Hollywood film and you will know what you have to do." said the attending psychiatrist after taking the medical history of his patient, Vikas Verma.

"I will….I will...," nodded Vinita.

"Good luck, take care, see you next week."

7

"Dedicated people have troubled married life; a man like you shouldn't marry." This came from Dr. D. P. Sharma, Professor of Veterinary Pathology. Dev too believed being single was best for his eccentric life style. Not eating in hostel mess. Living most of the time on fruits, raw vegetables and snacks. How the lady he marries, would react to his eccentricity? Yet, nature is intrinsically feminine. Woman is part of life, even as sages and seers have deemed her as barrier in their search for truth. Biological life cycle is incomplete without a woman. Not completing your life cycle; won't that be a significant loss?

In school days Dev was a movie buff. Often he wished 'the end' extended a bit to enable him see hero and heroine live in bliss. But the hall lights switched on and audience moved out. How he wished the story continued little more. His wife would love him like heroine loves hero on screen. He would miss out on this if he decides to remain bachelor.

Film 'Choti Si Mulakat' impressed him deeply. Boy and the girl get married in childhood, then there is time gap. They meet in college as grownups. Boy (Hero) recognizes the girl (this though is revealed at the end of the story) but girl doesn't, albeit she knows she was married to someone in her childhood. As college goers they fall in love. Story climaxes with the lady unable to decide which way to go, to the boy she had already married, or to her college love. Her late father's counsel resonated in background: when on cross roads, follow your conscience. Accordingly, she decides to go to the boy she had married, and knocks on a door. Her sister-in-law appears and runs back saying: maa, bahu aai hai (mother, your daughter-in-law has come)! Then walks in a man, clad in dhoti-kurta, and she is shocked to see him. He is the same, her college love.

"You should have told me," she cried on his shoulder, "that we were already married. Why did you make me suffer?" Embracing her, the hero said: "Sita must pass through her agnipariksha (a ritual to prove chastity by passing through smoldering fire, as done by Sita after she returned from the captivity of the demon king Ravan), the trial by fire."

The film ends with title song saying: I saw you, liked you, and worshiped you; that's all my fault, nothing else.

Growing up Dev had wished this film to continue beyond 'the end'. Why would a woman come in way of a man's search for truth? Woman stays loyal to her husband, come what may, so nothing wrong in getting married.

8

Dr. Mukesh reminisced about his daughter's disturbed married life.

Boy is highly suspicious and that irks my daughter. He is post graduate engineer, but behaves like a school boy. When he suffered nervous breakdown while doing his M.Tech, no dedicated treatment was given to him. All that Col. Verma did was advise him to drop M.Tech and sit at home. Vikas wisely decided to continue his studies, encouraged by his friends. Now Ramjilal University has sacked him saying he suffers from acute Schizophrenia. I understand Schizophrenia is extremely difficult to cure. I met his Professors before finalizing the marriage. None of them told me any such thing. They said Vikas was a brilliant scholar.

Vikas was fussy and argued on trivial matters. Why you took so long in bathroom? Why you did not wish my senior? Why did you laugh at my cousin sister? Saying sorry was best way out for the young bride. Vinita did just that and waited for matters to improve in course of time.

One day, post-midnight, Vinita was woken up by a rude shake. It was Vikas, his breath smelling of alcohol. She suppressed anger but Vikas caught her emotion and felt sorry. His friends forced him to drink, he said. "It's alright," said Vinita fighting her stupor and resting her head back on pillow.

Dev heard Mukesh patiently and consoled him. He understood the pain of Prajapati family. His own sister was forced to leave her in-law's home and live with her parents. Nothing lasts, he advised Mukesh, neither the good times, nor the bad ones. God has blessed Mukesh with an intelligent and competent daughter like Vinita. He should have faith in Vinita's ability to solve her problems.

"Why do people marry? Is it a social necessity, biological need, or both?" was being discussed in hostel. Most opined that it was a biological need. Dev disagreed. It was social necessity, not a biological one, he said.

"So you mean to say one can remain a celibate, a *brahmchari,* whole life?"

"Yes, why not?"

"Say about yourself, are you a celibate?"

"No I am not. But I do try to be one. Sexual purity is difficult, but it isworth trying for."

"If a dedicated man like you fails, then surely it must be impossible."

"Who told you I am dedicated…" said Dev, "…I am not. I don't fall into the category of the really committed and dedicated people. Sex is an outlet of chaos within as well as outside of the human body. Some succeed in controlling the within chaos, some outside. Controlling both is like riding two horses at a time. Children grow up hearing cuss words, innuendoes and insinuations with sexual overtones. That is the chaos outside. Hormonal and physiological changes they encounter on the way to adulthood are the chaos within. Children thus grow up riding two horses. Slips therefore are bound to happen."

"Heaven on earth can be felt in three things…," said Dr. Kunwar Pal Singh, "… in the pages of a book, on the back of a horse and in the arms of a woman."

"Yes," observed Dev, "that's an Arabian saying. Heaven lies in her arms, not the nether region. Male of Bolinia worm lives in the genital track of the female. Man shouldn't." House was in splits.

A man saw his wife in labor and developed aversion for sex, said Dr. Garg. Wife informed her sister who decided to mend him. She took him to a pond covered with green algae and threw a stone in. Ripples formed in water tearing green surface into two parts. As water stilled, split green sheet closed in and became a continuous green cover once again.

"Do you understand this?" asked sister-in-law. The man understood.

9

"Yes celibacy can lead to longevity but only when the idea comes from within. Not first analyzing and then going (for it)." Dr. V. K. Shrivastav, teaching reproductive physiology, was answering a query from Dev Purohit.

"What happens to millions of sperms that remain stored in body if not expelled out?"

"These disintegrate and get absorbed into the living system. Sex cells are destined to perish any way. Only a single sperm finally qualifies to form a new life, rest of the sperms die and disintegrate."

"What about weakness that follows sexual intercourse?"

"Is that your personal experience?"

Class laughed loud as Dev looked sideways embarrassed.

"Indeed, general perception is," continued Dr. Shrivastav, "that sexual activity leads to drop in energy level. Answer is yes and no. `Yes' because for each peak of excitement, there is bound to be an equal and opposite low. This is law of action and reaction. `No' because sexual arousal is a state of disturbance which, generally, can't subside without orgasm. Mating and ejaculating removes disturbance and you can concentrate on something more meaningful. That way it is an energizing and refreshing experience. A glass of milk after the act adequately compensates for the loss of proteins in sexual discharge. Low down felt after coitus is also psychological to some extent as we grow up linking sex to guilt. Sex education is still a taboo and hence the wide spread ignorance on sex issues."

Man is lot more than flesh and bone. Victory over carnal desires is passport to heights of spiritualism. Atmosphere that raises us, conditions our mind. Youth get drawn to sex hearing lewd talks and living with the sexually hungry relatives and friends. Dev was abused when all of 9 years. Those who defiled him were family. "My neurons got fired rather early," Dev explained," hence celibacy is difficult for me. Yet I pursue it, because it's a tough target."

"How can you be a celibate as long as you live in main stream society? Go to a jungle and become a monk if you really want freedom from sex," said Ram Gopal, adding, "you can't become a Buddha without renouncing this world."

"Perhaps I can," responded Dev.

10

There is nothing wrong with me. Why are you taking me to Doctor?" Vikas shouted at Vinita.

The lady cajoled and pampered him but failed. Finally she lost her temper. Did he not remember their last visit to the doctor!? Second visit was due today. That infuriated Vikas, and he hit her. Her upper lip swelled with injury. Realizing enormity of what he did, Vikas recoiled: "Sorry, sorry Vinita, extremely sorry," he pleaded, "You know Vinita I love you."

"That's like a good boy," smiled the bruised lady, "now follow me."

A beeline of patients waited in psychiatric clinic of Dr. A. K. Aggarwal. They took their seat. When called, they entered doctor's cabin.

"How are you Vinita? What happened to your lip?" asked Dr. Aggarwal.

"Nothing Doctor, I slipped in the kitchen," said Vinita, a little embarrassed.

"Is it so, young man?" Doctor looked hard at Vikas.

Vikas was flummoxed, guilt writ large on his face. Dr. Aggarwal was quick on damage control, "it seems you don't help your wife in kitchen, anyway, relax and get ready to answer my questions."

"OK Doctor." Vikas cleared his throat.

"Tell me about your most painful memory till date."

"I guess when I failed in ICS exam. I felt as if hit by a lightning. I thought someone deliberately failed me. I asked my father if ICS copies could be re-checked. He laughed wondering whether I had gone nuts."

"I see. Any other incident?"

"For my post-graduation I was denied scholarship in spite of highest aggregate marks. Reason cited was that I got supplementary in one subject. I pleaded that one supplementary should not pull down my overall academic merit, including 2nd merit position in final term. But my request was turned down.”

“How did you feel then?”

“I felt numb all over my body, cold in extremities. It was summer time. I felt strange disconnect with my body. I tried to see if I could move my hands, legs and fingers. I could indeed move them as I wished and that came as immense relief.”

Dr. Aggarwal requested Vinita to leave the two of them for a one on one. There were some questions which could best be asked and answered in her absence. Vinita walked out.

11

Tej Ram Tomar had a flourishing real estate business. Called bhaiya ji in professional circle, as well as in family, he dropped studies after 10+2 and started assisting his late father Ramjilal Tomar in the business.

Ramjilal University, Baghpat, Uttar Pradesh was his new venture. University had only 1200 students against expected 4000. To complicate matters, thousands of fake certificates with the University logo were confiscated by the Crime Branch of Police from various places all over India.

Educational documents came to University in huge numbers, by post and emails, to be verified for genuineness. Officials from Education Department of the state of Punjab visited personally with a bundle of documents. These were submitted by the candidates who had cleared the examination held for recruitment of primary school teachers for the government schools in Punjab. They would join duty only if their educational degrees were found to be genuine. Vikas, Asst. Registrar, verified them, and was surprised to find that all of them were fake. He had a casual conversation with the officials over a cup of tea. "How is it that these candidates with fake degrees could clear your selection process for teacher's job?" Visitors had no direct answer. A senior in them remarked that Education Department of Punjab has nevertheless come of age. Earlier, documents used to be verified after teachers joined duty. Now verification is being done prior to their joining.

A brother-sister couple came from Jammu-Kashmir. Sister had a fake M.Phil degree. Why did they go for the fake? Girl was silent. Brother said, "Sister's marriage was being negotiated. They wanted M.Phil girl. An acquaintance promised us the degree for 2 lakhs. Now he is untraceable. We lost money as well as our honour."

Fake Degrees have a great demand in the matrimonial market.

If only guardians cared more for learning than degree, fakes won't have place in a civil society. A father came for verification of his son's mark sheets. Didn't he know that his son never studied in the

University, never took exams? Father agreed he did know that. Then why didn't he counsel his son and mend his ways? No answer.

Countless people find jobs riding on fakes. One showed himself as Brahmin and joined Army as a soldier. Actually he was a Yadav. Physical parameters demanded of a Brahmin are less compared to that from a Yadav. In course of time his real identity came to the notice of his superiors but no action was taken. Reason: there were many other fakes in that regiment. Taking action against one would open a Pandora's Box. The fake Brahmin is a pensioner now.

12

"Mid-way is a misquoted and misunderstood phrase. Like I can't run 10 Kms so let me walk the distance. But perfection that comes by run can't come by walk. Mid way is a compromise, an alibi. Buddha couldn't fast, go without food, for long. Hunger reduced him to bones. A girl offered him rice pudding. A starving Buddha ate pudding and felt good and propounded mid-way, a departure from extreme discipline of the saints and seers of his time."

"So?" Asked Mukesh listening intently to Dev over a peg of whisky. The two were attending the marriage ceremony of a common friend.

"So, mid-way is being used by common man to avoid peak discipline. Almost everyone can have his or her own mid-way. Vikas, in my opinion, is stuck mid-way."

"What do you mean?"

"If Vikas suspects an insider hand in fake degree racket, he must be right."

"Should I ask him to turn approver to the investigating agencies?"

"No. He doesn't have a concrete proof. Gossip is not evidence. Vikas must wait for the right opportunity."

"University is supposed to be beacon light for society. And here it is, spreading deceit. O my God!"

"Society is more to blame for fake degrees than University. Veena, my own daughter failed in Maths. She failed even the supplementary exam. Someone advised her to buy a pass certificate for Rupees 5000/- and move on to next higher class, eleventh. Two of her friends bought forged certificates. Veena pined for same but I refused outright. Study math for 1 year, I said. I won't mind her failing even after a repeat of one year. No shortcut, I said. She passed Math after 1 year of dedicated study. Now she is Senior Manager in a multinational company."

"Many professionals, Bank Officers, PSU employees, Lawyers, and one 2nd Lieutenant in Indian Army, got sacked following verification of their documents."

"They asked for it. They fell to the charm of mid-way, short cut."

"The only solution to this problem is that parents teach their children to become good human beings, and not professionals with fat earnings."

13

"As a veterinarian you can't hope to be very rich. But there is no lack of professional opportunities. Remember, revolutions begin from middle class, never from top. May be one of you begins a revolution in medicine."

This was fresher's day advice from Dr. B P Joshi, Professor of Veterinary Medicine to the fresher batch of B.V.Sc & A.H students.

While referring to revolution, Dr. Joshi had Dev Purohit in mind. Delivering speech on Gandhi Jayanti, 2nd October, Dev quoted Gandhiji to slur modern medicine. Allopathy blames microbes for disease, he said, but it is not true. Microbes are innocent bystanders in disease environment.

Audience included bacteriologists, virologists and other experts of veterinary science. There was pin drop silence as Dev finished his talk. Dean of College, Dr. Bhardwaj, craned his neck to have a fulsome view of Purohit, the new admission. Post event, Dr. Joshi asked Dev: why are you so much against modern medicine?

Dev had a bone to pick with modern medicine. As a child he suffered from smallpox, fevers, ear aches and many other ailments. As a teenager he was pale and weak. Nocturnal emissions, or night falls were a regular feature. All this in spite of his visit to many doctors. Finally he decided to be his own guide. He searched and researched on health. Semen, said one book, was repository of masculine power. Losing it meant losing strength, physical and mental. One must spend all energy before going to bed. Otherwise the stored energy escapes through sexy dreams.

Another book titled 'Diet Reform- the way to Health and Vitality' changed his life forever. It talked about Naturopathy, about living close to nature. And Dev never looked back.

Doctors' livelihood depends on sale of medicines, said author of the book, adding, "But I don't depend on the sale of this book. So I can afford to tell you the truth." Book eulogized raw eating. Eating cooked food is ignorance if not stupidity. Author himself suffered host of ailments, and all medical treatments he took, failed. Then he stumbled on Nature Cure and went on a weeklong fast supervised by Naturopathic Doctor. When it was time to beak the fast, author was feeling so well that he wished to continue fasting a bit more. Naturopath was amused but insisted that breaking the fast was as important as going for it in the first place.

Dev's mother used to observe fast as religious ritual. Dev had once fasted along with his mother on the occasion of Shivratri. He was asleep when mother woke him up to break his fast at mid night. He had no hunger and wished to continue sleeping. He hadn't eaten during the day, yet he had no hunger. As mother insisted, he ate mechanically. For the next three days he was unwell. Fasting was not a happy memory with Dev. But going hungry for health was new knowledge for him and he must test it. He went ahead on an unsupervised fast of 3 days.

What struck him, at the end of fasting, was black foul smelling stools on day 3rd. It was a great relief at physical level, and he wondered if it was that foul matter which made him ill and ridding it was why he felt good. Thereafter eating sparingly, only one square meal a day, became a habit with him. Skipping meals, restricting chapatti intake to 3 and gorging on vegetables helped him. Tea gave him a high in low energy phase of long and short fast. He tried to give up tea, as advised in nature cure, but failed. Compromise with tea suited him.

The new found knowledge made him a fussy eater.

Dev read extensively on nature cure. Fasting became a habit with him. Fruit juice and veggies were his staple diet. How can you live without eating rice and chapattis? Asked his parents. But results were there for all to see and he was a picture of good health in no time. A school mate remarked: look Dev has become healthy by reading books on health.

Dev delved more and more into nature cure and natural living. As a child he was greatly inspired by stories of revolution and social reforms. Health was one area where revolution was required. He resolved to be a revolution on health front.

In college hostel Dev took only one meal - lunch. To his surprised colleagues he said: A normal person eats twice, a sick man thrice, but Yogi- only once. In time even one staple meal seemed monotonous. Dev wanted to move ahead of cooked food, and eat all raw. When will he go for absolute diet reform if not now, at the age of 20? With one firm resolve, he jumped into unknown waters.

Dev's once a day eating was queer enough for his colleagues. That he has given up even on one-time conventional food, would not be received well by his family and friends. So, he worked on a secret plan. There were many eating joints within and outside of hostel. When asked as to where he ate, he gave dodging answers. Telling the truth was avoided for 2 reasons: one- it would invite more questions, two- if he failed on all raw diet, he would quietly return to conventional eating.

Eating raw wasn't easy. He relied excessively on snacks and tea, lost weight, but remained upbeat.

Dev passed graduation and got admitted to PG program. Subject chosen was Veterinary Pathology. Admission committee asked: you got highest marks in Gynecology, then why have you chosen pathology?

"I am interested in Pathology." Dev replied.

Hostel was abuzz with speculations. Gynecology trashed for Pathology? Gynecology is more prospective. Many want to go for Gynecology, but don't get admission in this subject. And here is Dev, missing this great chance. Perhaps he wants to prove that germs don't cause disease. What does he think of himself? Scientists are fool, Pharmacy is farce. Only Dev is right, naturopathy is right. He must be crazy.

14

"Vikas I have talked with your colleagues. Your fears of a conspiracy against you are real, not mental disease. I will tell this to your doctor." Vinita spoke with an air of conviction.

Vikas was surprised. For the past 1 year he sensed that management of University was pitted against him, but why and how he could never work out. Vinita revealed how Dr. Badri Nath Tiwari, the ex-VC, was hand in glove with Harender Singh, the middleman for sale of fake certificates. Together they sold fake certificates of Diploma in Computer Applications (DCA). Signatures of Vikas were planted on these Certificates. Dr. Tiwari schemed to declare him a case of Schizophrenia so that the case of DCA fakes is closed once for all with the sacking of Vikas.

Ramjilal University never conducted DCA course. But many candidates recruited to State Transport Department of Rajasthan claimed they studied for DCA at Ramjilal University. Their educational certificates carried signatures of Vikas Verma. Dr. Tiwari had called for Vikas and asked him: is this your signature?

"Yes."

"How come?'

With pounding heart Vikas had asked for the original copy of document.

"Crime branch has confiscated originals for forensic examination."

An enquiry committee was constituted by Dr. Tiwari to investigate the matter. Committee passed that Vikas signed on fake certificates for pecuniary benefits. Dr.Tiwari grilled Vikas in his office. It is a bundle of lies, submitted Vikas. VC suggested that Vikas should resign or be prepared to be sacked. If Vikas agreed to resign, Dr. Tiwari could help him with placement in Manas Vidyapeeth where he had connections. A livid Vikas shouted at him: "to hell with your job offer!"

Tiwari called for security man who tried to shove him out of VC's office. Incensed Vikas caught him by the neck and boxed him in face. Bleeding from nose, the security man stood sheepishly in one corner.

Call more of your men; one is not enough, said Vikas looking menacingly at VC. A shaken Tiwari called for Police. Cops came and took Vikas away.

Vikas woke up to a head tap by Vinita, "hi, where are you? I am talking and talking and you are not listening."

"Sorry', Vikas woke up from flashback, "I slipped into a past memory. Please continue."

"OK, I was saying I talked to Dr. Navnit Jat, Dean Academics. He said that ex-VC Dr. Tiwari, Harender Singh and our Chancellor Bhaiya Ji were directly involved in sale of DCA mark sheets. Jat refused to reveal more but said he was anguished that such things are happening in University. He is trying to switch job and will quit Ramjilal as and when he finds a suitable job."

"Vinita, I took care to see all documents before signing them. But at one point a big heap of mark sheets piled on my table. I signed mechanically to dispense them. I fear someone might have pushed fakes into that heap and I ended up signing them in hurry."

"Bona fide mistake happen even in Prime Minister's Office."

"But I had nightmares on this count. Many who I suspect of deceiving me ran away without resigning. Some were sacked. I remained on chair to face consequences for crime I never did."

"I know you went into deep depression and shouted obscenities. And then you were in psychiatric care for long where Psychiatrist was bribed by Dr. Tiwari to declare you a case of Schizophrenia."

"Thank God, I can breathe easy now."

15

Dr. Dev Purohit and Dr. Sudhir Patil were misfits at Punjab Hatcheries, Ludhiana, a unit of Eggbro International, Pune, Maharashtra. So, both were transferred to a fledgling new project, Doon Hatcheries, Dehradun.

Dev was notorious for naturopathic advice. Chief Pathologist Dr. Prabhakaran prescribed some medication for a layer farm. Dev countered it. Farm was beset with high mortality and low production. Sukhdev, the owner was crestfallen. Bankers were breathing on his neck. His poultry farm was running in huge loss and the only way he could repay bank loan was by selling his farm assets. He gave SOS call to Dev who rushed to meet him.

Sukhdev was high on drink. "Have a peg Doctor." he said trying to get up and then giving up mid-way.

"No thanks," Dev said. "Be cool Sukhdev. This is not the time for boozing. You must do something out-of-the-box."

"No way doctor,' said Sukhdev, "I am closing down, can't put up with more losses. A chain of doctors and poultry experts have failed to solve my problem. Medicine bill alone is a whopping 5 lakhs. How can I survive? You are a doctor. I challenge you. Cure my birds. Stop mortality at my farm. Can you do it? You people are hypocrites, never take a challenge."

"Don't challenge me Sukhdev," said Purohit, "all you have to do is to stop current treatment, including the latest by Dr. Prabhakaran. Put your birds on plain drinking water. Let birds choose what to eat. Put grains and cakes in separate feeders. Keep finely chaffed green fodder as well."

"OK I will do it. Will it stop mortality?'

"Did you ask same question to other doctors?'

"No."

"Then why to me? You spent lakhs on medicines. Can't you try my advice which costs nil?'

"How can there be a cure without medicines?'

"Did spending 5 lakhs on medicines save your birds? I have no answer to `how'. You can either accept my advice or reject it."

Sukhdev was in no mood to try Dev's naturopathic advice. He sold his farm and returned to his business of fruits and vegetables in Mumbai. Word spread that Dr. Dev trashed advice of Chief Pathologist Dr. Prabhakaran. Before leaving for Mumbai, Sukhdev went to Punjab Hatcheries office and shouted obscenities. "You gave me poor quality birds." He thundered, "Your Doctors are fools, they destroyed my farm. You all are a bunch of liars and cheats."

Dev had tested nature-cure on his own self. If he could benefit from it, so could birds and animals. He was fond of saying, "no treatment (with drugs and medicines) is also a treatment." He was served show cause notice several times for prescribing fasting, milk and vegetable juice to birds. Dr. Prabhakaran was fed up. There was no point in calling explanation one more time. Dev was just handed a crisp memo saying: Transferred to Dehradun with immediate effect.

Dr. Sudhir Patil met Dev in the evening, cursing Prabhakaran.

"They are accusing me of taking bribe in the purchase of maize" moaned Patil. "I chose costlier maize because of quality. The cheaper grain showed fungal growth. I have the lab report, but they are not listening to me and say I have taken money in the deal."

Patil was also transferred to Dehradun with immediate effect. His plea that his son's academic year would be effected wasn't accepted. Both Dev and Sudhir must report at Doon Hatcheries within a week's time.

16

Sita Ram, SHO Baghpat, reached University with the result of forensic report. Report said that the signatures on fake Certificates were laser print, not hand signed.

Vinita was thrilled by the news and rushed home to inform Vikas. Some of her colleagues were already there, congratulating Vikas. She thanked visitors profusely and announced: "Please come for dinner, we will celebrate it in a big way."

Dr. P.C. Yadav, the new VC who took charge after Dr.Tiwari, welcomed Vikas in his office and personally handed him reinstatement letter. Vikas would report duty as Asst. Registrar with immediate effect.

With the arrival of Dr. Yadav, there was a breeze of fresh air in campus. Doctorate in agriculture, Dr. Yadav closely inspected saplings and plants sown in campus. Weak and bent plants were pulled into shape by rope tug. Annual sports were held in a big way. He accepted proposals for Interuniversity games and competitions. Campus was buzzing with activity all over.

Vikas informed VC that marketing team was fetching admissions through unfair means. They made false promises to candidates, creating problem for the University administration. One student on joining hostel asked for pillow and bed sheets. When informed that these had to be arranged by students themselves, he became livid and said he was assured by marketing team that pillow and bed sheet would be provided to him by the University. Sometimes they promise unthinkable. Like surety of passing in examination. "Tell me sir, how can a teacher pass a student who is failing?"

VC called for a meeting of teaching staff and the marketing team. There were glaring differences in their perception of how to attract   admissions for the University. Pressure of target notwithstanding, false promises shouldn't be made, VC asserted.

Marketing team complained that teaching staff wasn't giving honest feedback. Teachers cribbed that marketing staff showed them down in appraisal meetings. "They have only one job, of bringing admissions. Our primary job is to teach, and bringing admissions is secondary." Remarked a senior faculty.

17

Having heard Vinita patiently, Dr. Aggarwal wiped his specs, took a deep breath and said: "Vikas is a case of Neurasthenia (nervous breakdown), not schizophrenia."

Dr. Aggarwal had talked to Col. K.K. Verma and his wife in great details and concluded that Vikas, their only child, grew up emotionally deprived. He grew up believing that his father must be obeyed - come what may. He needs to be mainstreamed into society with regular counseling. Fear of failure dogs him consistently. One can fail even with sincere efforts. He must realize that he owes duty not only to his father and mother, but also to other members of society. Injustice happens to all in some way or the other. One commits suicide, another loses his bearing and a third person moves forward taking failure in stride. Vikas is second category and must graduate to third category.

"Kindly give me your diagnosis in writing. I need this to counter earlier medical report kept in his personal file." Said Vinita.

"Yes I will."

"What about medication?"

"Here is a new prescription. Only one medicine is to be given at bed time. Take him to parties, get-togethers, picnics. No need to confine him to home or watch his behavior."

18

The idea of Ramjilal University was conceived in a casual talk. One day Sajag Arora, the younger son-in-law of Tej Ram Tomar proposed to him: "Papa why don't you start a University."

"Well I did think of starting a school. But University….ah….no…."

"Why?'

"I guess breakeven for a University is long, 15 years. It is a massive expenditure. I can't feed a project for so long."

"What if it breaks even in just three years?'

"You must be joking."

"I am not."

"Then come to me tomorrow with a detailed project report."

Sajag was dot on time. He remained closeted with BhaiyaJi for 3 long hours. Proposal was so gripping that the two stayed glued to each other. No water, no tea. When Tejram took break, he asked for tea. After tea, the two again sat down to discuss risk factors.

"Fake Certificates will not be sold to every Tom Dick and Harry. They will be sold to select people only. Especially to those whose names would be similar to our regular students. Similarity of names is bound to increase as our admission would go up. Such names can be verified true even if they are not. In course of time fakes would be adjusted as regulars in University record." Explained Sajag.

Akanksha, Tejram's younger daughter and Sajag's wife, walked in. Sajag had briefed her on University project, except fake degree part. The two decided to send her back as further talks wouldn't be possible in her presence. Could she arrange for tea and snacks for them? Yes, why not, said Akanksha.

"But our employees will get an air of it." Tejram reflected on a serious note.

"So what? Employee turnover would be a whirlwind. Hire and fire ruthlessly. Employees are slaves, and must be forced to think and act like slaves. If they smart up, fire them. No appointment letters for them till they prove their loyalty."

Bhaiya Ji approved the idea. He would give his father's name to this project - Ramjilal University. One last question, "Have you discussed this idea with my elder daughter Prateeksha and her husband Jitendra Singh?'

"Yes Papa,' said Sajag, "I have discussed everything with them sans one issue, that of Fake Certificates."

"That's sensible."

"Jitendra and Prateeksha are dedicated employees in private firms. They are idealistic and have no hands on experience of business. In course of time I will bring them around to this issue, gently."

"What about Akanksha, your wife?'

"She is also idealistic but understands that cheating is part of business. If I find her in right frame of mind, I will tell her also."

"But I believe we should keep it a secret from all three of them. Thanks to my wife Shanti, they live in a balloon of idealism."

19

Tejram had some doubts over salability of fake certificates. To convince him, Sajag took him to Manas Vidyapeeth, paid 1 Lakh in cash and bought a BA degree for Bhaiyaji.

Procedure was simple. Tejram signed on a pile of blank answer sheets, submitted his class 12th Certificates, passport size photographs and an affidavit that gap in his education was because of his venturing into family business, not because of any illegal or immoral activity. Rest of the job would be done by Vidyapeeth. Meticulous paper work would show that Bhaiya Ji attended all regular classes and appeared for all exams of his 3 year Bachelor of Arts degree.

Tejram was assured that degree given to him was valid in every way and Vidyapeeth would pay double the amount, i.e. 2 lakh rupees, to anyone who could prove it fake. Wow! What a business! If a little paperwork could churn out so much of money, then there couldn't be a better business than starting a University.

I am not doing anything wrong, thought Bhaiya Ji. Countless teachers and government servants ride on forged degrees. Many pass exams by hiring proxy. One runs a sham newspaper. Circulation is shown as 3 lakhs per day whereas only a few hundred copies are actually sold. A lineman of Electricity department lives in a massive bungalow. Can values win a decent life in India? No. I ran from pillar to post for my construction projects and bribed all from bottom to the top in Government offices. Corruption is a way of life in India. If you are not in it, you lose business.

There is a big market for fakes in India. Who will guard the guards? If fake graduates find jobs, employer is to blame. Many get caught, punished, fired. Well they asked for it. For seller it's a safe business. Buyers can't go to court as they are equal partners in the crime. Hence business of fake documents thrives unchecked.

The dye was cast. Tej went all out to establish Ramjilal University.

20

"Imagine a Doctor, Engineer, Army Officer, policeman or any x y z with a fake degree. What do you expect? They have already sold their soul, how can they serve the nation? They can only be a parasite on society."

PP (Purohit Prajapati) duo sat pondering in a get together.

"My earliest memory of cheating goes back to class 2. Boy sitting in front of me was being prompted by teacher himself." Said Dev.

"Ajeet Pal of our batch knew nothing, did nothing and cheated in all exams.   He not only did graduation but even post-graduation, all by cheating."

"Yes, he was pretty envied for this. Ideally his degree shouldn't be rated genuine. It is as bad as fake. But practically speaking, his degree gave me a good career."

"Yes,' laughed Mukesh, "But he was very social and kept obliging teaching faculty in some way or the other; not everyone can do that."

"Smaller fish like Aslam and Ravinder failed and repeated academic year. Ajeet never failed. And Akash, the topper of our batch had to serve under Ajeet Pal in Animal Husbandry department."

"One iconic scholar of my village, Lecturer in a Government College, and due for promotion, was eliminated by a rival group of teachers."

"O my God!'

"He was stopped on way. His wife pleaded: take my jewelry, all money we have, we can pay more- please spare my husband's life. Killers didn't relent. Life of her husband was all they wanted."

"Environment that exists in our society is conducive for fake degrees and fake professionals. Corruption in public life has boosted this market. Generation that grew on fakes passed on the baton to the next generation. Now it has become a self-perpetuating cycle."

"Right, I am myself a victim of one fake myself."

Mukesh looked on puzzled. Dev clarified: "I married a girl with fake degree. Her father was a school teacher. She was a subnormal child but her father forced her to be a graduate. All for one purpose – to get her married decently."

"You mean to tell me that your marriage didn't work because of fake degree?'

"Yes. My wife had a disturbed childhood. She suffered from infection of internal ear which was ignored. She was poor in studies all through. Her father bailed her out. But he couldn't bail her out of a disturbed married life though he tried hard. I suffered collateral damage."

21

Construction work of Ramjilal University began in top gear. Purchase of the land near bank of river Yamuna, clearance from the State Government, printing of Mark Sheets began simultaneously.

Printing of Mark sheets was demanded by Harendra Singh (HS), the linkman to fake degree from-any-university. Tej was amused. Teaching work hasn't begun and here was HS with bagful of money. He wanted a thousand mark sheets of different subjects. What a deal!

Tejram commanded his cousin Sompal Tomar, "I want a functional University in just one year!'

Sompal retired as Principal from a Government School and was promised job of 'Dean Administration' in Ramjilal University. He got on with the job as instructed. Contractors, Drivers and Engineers who sought work in the construction project must give at least one admission to the University when academic session begins. A security of Rs.20, 000/-was deducted from their wages. If they bring admission to university, the security shall be returned to them. If not, they will lose their deposit of Rs.20, 000/-.

It was year 2008. World was reeling under economic slowdown. Unemployment was all-time high. Most workers agreed to bring admissions in order to get job. Soon Ramjilal University was buzz word in the area, thanks to publicity by workforce to save their Rs. 20, 000/- deposit.

Academic year of the University began in December 2008. Construction work was still incomplete. Some 100 odd admissions were accommodated in partially finished hostel building. Teaching and non-teaching staff was appointed on same condition: bring admission or lose your security of Rs. 20,000/-.

Fakes, in the meanwhile, were selling like hot cakes. Money collected was spent in publicity work of the newly established 'world class' University. Lavish parties were organized for officers of State Administration and Education Department. Nearest Police Thana was pampered. A clerk in Education Department wanted a fake for his niece; got it. A High Court Judge wanted his ward to do LLM. Ward was admitted even as permission to start law courses was still awaited. Three years later Judge would create ruckus forcing University to return the entire fee that his ward had paid.

Fast turnover of teaching faculty reflected on quality of teaching work. Bhaiyaji hired and fired ruthlessly. Fakes were producing a steady cash flow for University as well as for his Construction business. Soon, the underbelly of Ramjilal was known to all. One could go there for regular course, or buy a degree. Conscientious parents kept away from University. Those wanting quick jobs with fakes, approached an ever obliging HS, bought fake degrees, and found jobs.

22

Second academic session of Ramjilal attracted 500 admissions. Target of 2000 was unachievable. A worried Bhaiyaji called for a meeting with VC Dr. B N Tiwari and the teaching staff - 60 in number.

"How can I pay your salaries if there are no admissions?' began Tejram. "My marketing team is running around. But that alone will not help. Each one of you in teaching and supporting staff must get me 10 admissions, be it from your relatives, friends or whatever."

Bar of 1 admission was suddenly raised to 10. All in meeting kept mum. To counter Chancellor meant loosing job. Blue print of how-to-bring-admissions was laid out. Teachers must move out and contact educational institutions. Vehicles would be provided by the University. Meet relatives, teachers, friends, acquaintances, coaching institutes and bring admissions. Career prospect in Ramjilal is linked to admissions procured. Those who can't bring admissions must resign and pursue some other career. One senior teacher got up to ask a question, but hesitated.

"Yes go ahead." Said Tejram.

"Chancellor Sahb…"

"Don't call me Chancellor Sahb. Call me Bhaiyaji, all from peon to VC, please call me Bhaiya ji."

"OK Bhaiya Ji, if teachers go hunting for admissions, quality of teaching will go down. It will also reflect on overall discipline in campus."

"I will reply this,' said VC Dr. Tiwari. "See, I have already explained to you that 51% of your attention should be on academics and co-curricular activities, and 49% on other activities. This 49% of activity is related to admissions. We are not a government aided institution. Admissions are the only revenue we have. Admissions are our life line. If we don't get students in adequate number, who do we teach? And how do we meet daily expenses of running this university?

House was silent.

23

Dr. Dev Purohit, serving as Veterinary Officer at Doon Hatcheries, was called by the General Manager, A. K. Mathur. Dev must visit Manjushri Broiler Farm where chicks were dying in huge numbers. He must submit his report as soon as possible.

Dev spent entire working day at Manjushri and visited neighboring farms as well. He submitted a 4-page report which said supply of chicks to customers was biased. Good chicks and timely supply was given only to those who bribed sales team. The chicks supplied to Manjushri farm were less than scheduled number, as well as poor in quality.

"Dr. Prohit, are you trying to tell me that our Production Manager, Dr. Sudhir Patil is not doing his job?!' GM was visibly annoyed.

"You can have a one-to-one with Patil. I feel he, Sales Manager Rajinder Singh, and Hatchery Manager Venu Nair are hand in glove in exploiting poultry farmers. Raising temperature of Hatching Machine by 2 degrees above prescribed limit can ruin chick quality. It damages chicks at cellular level; grossly they appear normal. Damage at micro level causes high mortality at farmer's end. Postmortem of dead chicks reveals nothing significant. Insiders call it heat-up condition. Poultry professionals know that it is a vendetta weapon."

"What kind of revenge are we seeking from farmers?'

"Farmers who don't entertain Production and Sales staff are penalized with supply of heat-up chicks. Those who grease their palm, keep them in good humor with gifts, are rewarded with good chicks."

"And how do they temper with chick count?'

"Will a farmer supplied with 10 or 20 thousand chicks count every single bird on receiving his consignment? No. The delivery boy can easily fish out 100 chicks from each of 10 consignments being supplied, and make a new lot of a 1000 chicks. This lot is sold at a throwaway price. Against prevailing rate of 20/- per chick, any farmer will happily pay Rs15/- on spot. That makes kitty of Rs15000/-. Even our Accountant gets a share."

A livid GM immediately called for Dr. Sudhir Patil, Rajinder Singh and Venu Nair.

24

Ramjilal University hired a website 'Jockey' for office work on which all teaching faculty and the administrative staff registered their Ids. All internal and external communications were routed through this website. Apart from 'Jockey', employees worked on other portals like Google and yahoo. Airtel SIM was provided to all staff members of supervisor and above rank.

Third academic session was to begin in the month of August but admissions were abysmally low. Vacation was spent in admission hunt but results were discouraging. Vikas himself toured many schools and colleges lecturing on course offered, rebates given to girls, dependent of defense personnel, and ward of single parent. But the efforts didn't convert into admissions.

Bhaiya ji called for an appraisal Meeting. All were directed to deposit their Airtel SIMs with administration. These would be handed over to Admission Coordinators. Any call for admission on those numbers would be received by coordinators for necessary action. New SIM from a different company – Vodafone, were provided as replacement.

Teaching faculty must brace up for teaching and co-curricular activity of the current academic session, Bhaiya Ji announced. Admission coordinators will report on feedback received from areas visited by teaching faculty (for fetching new admissions).

Failing on admission target was dormant fear with all, teachers in particular. Students became pawns for admission hunt. They could hope for moon if they helped teacher get new admissions. A new dimension was added to teacher-taught relationship; now they were business partners.

A tug of war for admissions was palpable in Campus. Some drivers and attendants complained that the admissions they brought to University were high jacked by teachers and the marketing team. Those admissions were from their friends and relatives, and this could be verified. But in records they are shown as brought in by someone else. On the other hand, teachers blamed marketing staff for poaching on admissions which they had mobilized. Beg, borrow or steal became the way to meet admission targets.

Some admissions came direct to University through Advertisements and internet browsing. Such admissions too were tweaked to someone's credit. Security staff was quick to fish on innocent walk-ins. They were tactfully brainwashed and forwarded as brought-in by x y or z person. A chaos prevailed below the veneer of a Global University.

25

Vinita's married life was gradually coming on rails. She was 3 months into her pregnancy. Her parents were thrilled. There was a rider though. Vinita suffered from high blood pressure. She may not be able to carry baby to full term. Caesarian was indispensable. Mukesh was worried, so was Dev.

"Fetus is developing well, but I don't understand why caesarian is a foregone conclusion."

"The way things are, we can't argue with Doctors." responded Dev.

Into her 7th month, Vinita went for routine checkup. Doctors suspected some abnormality. She was rechecked and advised immediate caesarian. She was shocked, "But I still have a month and a half to go." Doctors persisted, "Delay can harm."

Vikas urged Vinita not to argue with Doctors but submit herself to surgery. Mukesh was informed that his daughter would undergo caesarian in an hour's time. Clock ticked heavily for Mukesh. Finally he got a call. "Congratulations, you have become Nana. It's a female baby." It was Vikas. Phone got disconnected, then it was live again. Caesarian went well. Mother and the baby are well. Message finally sunk in. A milestone was reached. Mukesh became grandfather. See how time flies, he thought.

Dev congratulated both families. Name the new born Adheera (meaning impatient), he suggested, as it was impatient to come into this world, just in 7 and a half months. All laughed. But the name finalized was Aashi. Baby remained in incubator for one and a half months. Doing rounds of baby was hard time for her parents. In 2 months' time, baby was discharged from hospital.

26

CID officer Hema Ram called on Vikas in his office to enquire about Amit Sikera. He was close relative of Bhaiya Ji, said Vikas, and worked as store keeper in University. Being Chancellor's man, he was arrogant and hot headed.

"Why was he removed from service?" asked Hema Ram.

"He was having an affair with a B.Tech student. Ex-VC Dr. Tiwari caught him red handed and wanted him sacked, but Bhaiyaji didn't agree. VC put his foot down and threatened to resign if Amit was not sacked. Hence Bhaiya Ji was forced to sack Amit. This though was an eye wash because Amit was placed in Bhaiya Ji's construction business at Meerut."

"Why did Dr.Tiwari resign from University?'

"There are 2 theories regarding this. One that Amit lobby in University spied on VC, took photos of him in compromising position with a teaching faculty Deepa Seth. Deepa was old acquaintance of Tiwari and was appointed in University to start correspondence courses. She lived in staff quarter next to VC's residence. The other theory is that Dr. Tiwari had warned Bhaiya ji that his son-in-law Sajag was crossing limits. Business of fake documents must remain in manageable limits. But far from it, fakes were selling all over India, even abroad. Letters requesting verification of fakes piled up Like Mountain. That made him panic and resign."

"Can I see those letters?"

"No. They were burned down, as desired by Bhaiya Ji."

"Reminders must have followed, did you burn those too?"

"After several months we were forced to reply as we got reprimand from the Commissioner - Right to Information."

"How come your Chancellor abused `Right to Information'?"

"Well for long he believed right-to-information didn't apply to private sector. Now, thankfully he has come around."

Hema Ram left after paying courtesy visit to VC, Dr. P. C. Yadav.

27

Dev's report on Manjushri broiler farm brought Rajinder-Patil-Nair nexus into sharp focus. Rajinder Singh was sacked. Patil and Nair were spared with warning.

GM called Dev to his office. He didn't want to hire a new sales manager in place of Rajinder Singh. Will Dr. Dev agree to work as Sales manager? He will get a raise and related perks if he agreed.

"No problem Sir, but sales will need drastic overhauling."

"We will give you a free hand. Presently we are selling 1 lakh broiler chicks. I want you to up this figure to 2 lakhs per month. Give me your action plan. We will give you all facilities."

Dev moved in top gear. He recruited 2 sales representatives, Omkumar Yadav and Raj Saini. They moved in field area to sell company's broiler chicks without any discrimination between small, medium and big farmers. First come first served. For credit delivery, farmers must give Bank Guarantee. That forced Lala Ishwar Chand and Sardar Amarjit to meet Dev in his office.

"Doctor Sahab, are you angry with us?" The two spoke in chorus.

"Not at all. You are our esteemed customers. How can I be angry with you?"

"Then why have you stopped our credit supplies?"

"For credit supplies we need guarantee from your banker."

"Rajinder Singh gave us regular credit without any guarantee. We never defaulted on paying our dues."

"Don't tell me this. Rajinder Singh left a bad debt of 5 lacs, all in the name of you two. Apart from other things, this outstanding was reason why he was sacked."

"There was hatchery problem in chicks supplied to me on 3 occasions. Rajinder promised me compensation. I am still waiting for my compensation." Said Ishwarchand.

"Same happened with me." Added Amarjit.

"Hence you refused to pay your dues for supplies?" laughed Dev.

"Give us our compensation and we will clear the amount due to us."

"You are forcing your way on me. Rajinder Singh was not a doctor to have certified hatchery fault. He shouldn't have promised compensation without GM's approval. I can't work the way Rajinder did."

"Dr. Dev you must remember that we are opinion makers in Saharanpur. With this attitude you will not be able to sell a single chick in our area."

"Well in that case I will sell in Muzzafarnagar, Meerut, Najibabad and even in the state of Haryana and Delhi. And of course I will wait for you, our old customers, to return to our fold."

Meeting ended. They shook hands. Killer instinct was palpable in the veneer of courtesy.

28

When Dr. P.C. Yadav took over as Vice Chancellor, indiscipline prevailing in University shocked him. He called for personal files of 4 rowdy students.

One rowdy was son of an MLA. His father helped Tejram get ordinance for setting up the University passed in UP assembly. Student was caught red handed in girls' hostel and rusticated from Hostel. Girl in question was a psychiatric case. One teaching faculty got her admitted to University to meet his admission target. Girl didn't get admission in any college and her parents were worried. Teacher promised her parents he would get her admitted to Ramjilal.

Another, son of a builder in Dehradun, had submitted fake 12th pass certificate to get admitted in B.Tech program. His father was a friend of Tejram. He was now in final year of B.Tech program.

Third was a wayward son from a rich family. He lived Robin Hood style, giving generous tips to class 4 employees and roaming around the campus with his gang of goons. None, including teaching faculty dared check him.

Fourth was a close relative of Chancellor himself who seldom attended classes but got more than 80 percent marks in exams, courtesy direct orders from top.

Dr. Yadav made a case for these students and sent for Chancellor's approval. These students must be removed from University, he argued at length. For a month Chancellor sat on the proposal. Then sent file back with crisp note – proposal rejected. Reason was conveyed on phone. Student strength is already so poor. And here you are lowering it all the more.

Dr. Yadav got convinced that ills of University flowed from top. He was walking on a slippery road. His suspicion that Bhaiyaji was directly involved in sale of fakes grew by the day. Yet he was determined to do his best and reach to the bottom of problem. He called for Vikas and asked:"who manages Strong room?'

"Bhanu, the attendant."

"How can attendant be in-charge of strong room?" moaned Yadav. Registrar, Mr. Ruhil, was called and directed to produce Records of Strong Room. Ruhil shouted for Bhanu who came with a heap of files and Registers. Asst. Registrar, Vikas was also called in. Ruhil, the Registrar, had joined only a month back.

VC flipped through the Registers and his heart sank. Mark Sheets and Degree Sheets received from Printing Press were not entered in stock registers. Their issuing for use was also not recorded.

Ruhil looked blank. Four Registrars had come and gone before him. It was their job to have seen to this lacuna. Bhanu had nothing to say except that he did as he was directed, generally by Bhaiya Ji himself.

Strong Room is the heart of University, said a sobered Dr. Yadav. It must be kept under 3 locks with 3 senior officials directly monitoring it. Every time it is opened, an entry must be made in log book which all three officials must sign. That apart, entries in stock registers should be complete and kept updated in all respects.

29

Dr. Sudhir Patil called on Dr. Dev. A 3- day conference would be organized in Dehradun shortly. It would be attended by prominent poultry breeders of India. Some money, in number 2, must be raised for the show.

"How?'

"Sell chicks off record, on hard cash."

"New customers will ask for receipt."

"Then go to old customers."

"They will laugh at me. They have already challenged me to sell in their area. My boys are running day and night to meet this challenge. Now when we have made a new base, you want me to shift to old base. Not possible."

"But this is what GM wants. You can speak to GM."

Code for sale-without-receipt was `proforma' sale. Dev was privy to this clandestine activity at Ludhiana Office. It was a secret plan to raise black money. Dev once helped in proforma booking where chicks are booked against hard cash without issuing receipt for same. Sales team took him to a farmer who held him in high esteem. Farmer paid Rs. 5 lakhs cash for his next consignment of chicks. Sales team, as planned, feigned forgetting receipt book in office. "Don't worry about receipt, Kulwant," said Dev, "your money is in my pocket, prepare to receive your chicks tomorrow at 5a.m. sharp." Kulwant agreed, as he had complete faith in Dr. Dev. Sales team thanked Dev for helping them.

"Come in Dev," said GM seeing him from his office window.

Dev came straight to the point, "Sir I have two problems. One, we can't trust our salesmen with unaccounted cash. Second, farmers can blackmail us. Our ex-employee, Rajinder Singh now works in Skyline Hatcheries. He is selling chicks in Saharanpur. Thanks to him, farmers know about most of our covert operations."

"Then what should we do?"

"There are 10 farmers in my list who trust me blindly. I will approach them."

"Ever since I joined here I am being told how farmers have ditched us in past, that's very strange." Observed Mathur.

"We too have ditched farmers." Countered Dev. "There is an unwritten rule in company to find or invent fault at farmer's level. If mistake is on company's side, we must hide it to avoid paying compensation to farmer. Once I gave an honest appraisal of loss farmer suffered on account of bad chicks supplied by us. GM made faces saying if he approved such compensations, company will sink. I was a new comer then and my colleagues advised me against being pro-farmer."

"OK you can go ahead in whatever way you deem fit. But I need 50 lakhs in cash within a month for the Franchise meet."

30

Dr. Yadav was livid on phone. He was talking to Chancellor Tejram.

"How come you left strong room to the charge of an attendant. Stock Registers are incomplete. I wonder if fake mark sheets circulating outside were issued directly from our own strong room. There is no proper record of how many mark sheets and degree sheets got printed and how many got issued to students. How do I set this record straight?'

"You should contact Sompal Tomar for this information."

"Sompal says he doesn't know. Almost everything is in a mess. BOD meeting is never held and minutes of meeting are all cooked up. Academic Council hasn't met for the past 2 years. I just don't have a base line to work on. First inspection by UGC was a flop show. And application for second inspection is not yet prepared."

"You have been appointed to improve matters."

"I am sorry I can't. On top of it your son-in-law barges in University any time and insults my Pro VC who has resigned following face off with him. Why can't you restrain your son-in-law?"

"Henceforth he will not come to University, I have told him in clear terms."

"Even that doesn't solve my problem. I have evidence to show that he is involved in sale of fake certificates from the University Campus. An advocate of Rajasthan High Court paid 1 Lakh to Sajag for BA degree. That degree is verified as fake by Vikas Verma. Now he wants his money back. What do I tell him?'

"Let him file case against us. We already have 30 such legal cases. One more added to list won't make difference."

31

Mukesh Prajapati, Veterinary Officer in Kamdhenu Cooperative Milk Fedration, Lucknow, was posted at Meerut. Dr. Anuj Deswal, Artificial Insemination (AI) Officer called him to discuss about AI activities in Meerut zone.

Dr. Deswal was specialist in Animal Breeding. Prevailing conception rate in field was 3 for cows (3 inseminations required to make one cow pregnant) and 4 for buffaloes. He wanted it improved to 2 for cows and 3 for buffaloes.

A dairy farmer, Satpal Singh, complained about quality of the bull semen supplied in his village. Dr. Deswal packed his microscope and visited society. He inspected a few semen doses and found them OK. To convince Satpal, he showed him a drop of semen under the microscope. "Do you see some movement in this field?" he asked.

On way back he halted in a village where Mukesh was also present. Here too Dr. Deswal examined some semen doses and found them OK. Dr. Mukesh looked on flabbergasted and asked: "how can you examine without eye pieces?'

Eye pieces of the microscope lay in Dr. Deswal's office. He had forgotten to pack them. Office Attendant saw them lying on his table and telephoned to maingate to stop him, but by then Dr. Deswal was out."

Next day Milk Plant was abuzz with Deswal's faux passé. How could he examine semen doses with a microscope having no eye-piece? There were giggles and boisterous laughter. MD called AI Officer and asked him same question. Dr. Deswal was squarely shamed. For his Master's Degree he had used electron microscope. Did he then forget to use a lesser microscope? Dr.

Deswal was sacked and charge of AI handed over to Dr. Mukesh Prajapati.

32

"You know a bull never micturates (urinates) on ground" said Dr. K.C. Misra, Asst. Professor, Surgery, and the class was confused. Where else can it urinate if not on ground?

Pause was unusually long. Then came the answer. 'It micturates in the prepucial cavity."

Unlike man, prepuce of bull is a tunnel in abdominal wall. Penis remains coiled up behind this space in `S' shape. In sexual excitement `S' uncoils, and straightened penis comes out of the prepuce for coitus. After the act `S' re-forms, retracting penis back, leaving prepuce an empty space once again. Hence, in a normal state, bull urinates in this empty space, prepucial cavity, wherefrom the urine dribbles down to the ground.

Dr. Misra's lectures were full of wit and humor. Dissuading student from writing on slips of paper he said, "it is called slip because it slips". So one should always write in a notebook. Surgeons are the most soft spoken of all specialists, he said. They sit quietly in a debate, at the end of which, they quietly display the X-ray plate, and that would be the last word in Diagnosis.

In ancient India, higher knowledge was not available to all. Only deserving few got access to it. Then times changed, education opened for all. Did that make society any better?

You must develop your sensibilities, sense of touch, smell, taste, sight and hearing. That alone will make you a sound professional, said Dr. Dwedi, Professor of Pathology. In lymphoid leucosis, cutting the liver will give you a feeling of fullness. Mareck's Disease won't give that feeling. Now don't ask me what is feeling of fullness. Cut bird's liver with a knife on the post mortem table and `feel' it.

Adulterate milk in such a way that you don't get caught. That's what the subject of Dairying trains you for, observed a senior in Veterinary College. Indeed knowledge in hands of morally weak is dangerous. Education for all has pressured society. It has forced even the unwilling and undeserving to go for education. Naturally they resort to unfair means to pass exams. Fake degrees are part of this rat race. No wonder we have too many fakes around us.

33

Liquid nitrogen (LN2) had to be supplied to AI (Artificial Insemination) centers very urgently. If not done, semen doses kept in LN2 Containers would go bad. But there was a problem. LN2 couldn't be siphoned out from Primary Storage Tank as tap system failed. Tap was fitted well and due procedure was followed, but the super cooled liquid (minus 196 degree centigrade temperature), LN2, refused to come out.

Mukesh recalled how he used to siphon kerosene oil with a metallic pump. He brought a large sized kerosene pump, dipped it storage tank and moved piston up and down; LN2 flowed out in thick stream. He was overjoyed, but outpour suddenly stopped.

He removed the pump and found that its valve, a glass ball, was broken. Ball cracked because it couldn't bear the brunt of extreme cold (-196 degree Celsius). He replaced glass ball with steel ball; that solved the problem. Now liquid nitrogen flowed out uninterrupted as steel ball could bear the extreme temperature of Liquid Nitrogen.

Mukesh had another problem waiting in the wings. Calves born out of Artificial Insemination (AI) were week and mismatch with father bull. He visited some AI centers and was shocked to find that semen doses stored there were different than actually supplied. It transpired that the delivery boy was in collusion with a private breeder who swapped his poor quality semen with premium quality semen supplied by Federation.

Mukesh called a meeting of farmers and advised them to be vigilant. After getting their animals inseminated, they should keep the used `straw' for record. Straw, the PVC tube containing bull semen, must show Federation's signage. If no signage was found, they must report the matter.

34

Col. Ruhil, the Registrar, got unnerved by the mess in Ramjilal and resigned. Bhaiya Ji tried to hold him back but failed. Vikas, as usual, officiated as Registrar till a new Registrar could be appointed.

VC called for Vikas and had detailed discussion with him on University affairs. Things were moving from bad to worse. There were rumors that University was up for sale. Teaching staff was demoralized. What could be done?

"Sir, I don't know where to begin, but with every passing day there is a new revelation. People say more than 2000 million in Indian rupees is already collected through the sale of fake certificates. I got a call from a person named Sandeep that he personally handed over money to Bhaiyaji. Caller said he had proof with him and wondered why the sold degrees were not being verified as genuine, as true. When you have taken money, then you must verify them as valid, he repeated. I told him to talk directly to the Chancellor."

"My sources say more or less the same thing. Chancellor's reputation is all time low. His elder son-in-law, Jitendra, has filed for divorce. He believes his wife, Tejram's daughter, is part of syndicate selling fake degrees." Reflected VC Dr.Yadav

"O my God. I know Chancellor's elder daughter, Prateeksha. She did her MBA 2 years back from here only. Salary roster shows her as teaching faculty, as Associate Professor. She was selected in a multinational company and never worked in University. His younger daughter Akanksha did MBA from IIM Ahmadabad and is serving in America. She too is shown as Associate Professor in salary roaster. Both sisters draw Rs. 80,000/- per month from University even as the senior most teaching faculty doesn't get even half of this."

"I don't know how he is rotating money. His construction work at Meerut is in hot waters. A team of CBI grilled him for full 2 days on how he could go for a huge housing project without matching bank loan."

Dr. Yadav couldn't stay for long. Tired of having heated arguments with Chancellor on a daily basis, he walked out of University without formal resignation. Tejram phoned him to say that he must tender resignation else disciplinary action would be taken against him. An infuriated Yadav dared him to take disciplinary action. Bhaiyaji wisely decided not to do that.

35

Col K.K. Verma and his wife were finally repenting.

Breaking away from joint family made their son Vikas wayward. KK's acrimony with his father was known to all in his native village. Of his 2 brothers and 3 sisters, he took responsibility of only 1 brother, born of same mother as he. His mother died after giving birth to the 3 siblings, 2 sons and 1 daughter. Father remarried. Three siblings followed from step mother, one son and 2 daughters.

Vikas, KK's one and only son, was born in village. His mother, Kamala, a graduate, couldn't adjust in traditional joint family of his ancestral home in village Baleni of Baghpat. She nagged her husband, then 2nd lieutenant in India Army, to separate from joint family.

Village elders prevailed on KK to forgo his share of 5 acres of agriculture land to his father who had 3 siblings to look after. KK refused point blank. This was widely resented by villagers who believed the weaker members of family must be treated with grace. This made KK an outcast, a social misfit.

Depending on his father's posting, Vikas had his schooling at multiple locations. He was an average student, something that KK never liked: "You have 24 hours at your disposal," he said, "all for studies. When I was your age I did agricultural work and milked cows apart from studies. My scoring was same as yours, 50 percent. And I never took tuitions as you do." Such admonishment hit Vikas hard even as KK believed he said it in lighter vein.

Till 12 years of age Vikas grew up in Village Baleni, studying in Hindi medium school. His mother being arrogant and moody, part of her nature rubbed on to the growing Vikas. He had few friends and was prone to quarreling in school and outside.

Shifting from village to urban environment further complicated matters for Vikas. He had adjustment problem in English medium school and failed in class seventh.

36

To arrange for 50 lakh of hard cash, Dev approached his trusted farmer, Surender Malik who bought 50000 chicks every month. "May I choose you as buffer for our unsold chicks," he proposed. Malik agreed happily. OK then, explained Dev, I will give you credit supply of 20,000 chicks every month. You can pay for them after one month gap. Your interest is that you get chick without paying in advance and my interest is that I get a safe outlet for cancelled bookings and unsold chicks.

Surender agreed and requested if facility could be extended to 25,000 chicks instead of 20,000. May be in future, but not at the moment, said Purohit, and asked,"how about payment?'

"As you suggest." Said malik.

"Chicken seller Pawan Kumar of Dehradun buys your chicks. We will collect cash payment directly from him."

"OK. I will tell Pawan to pay you in cash."

Dev created way for 30 lakh hard cash. And called meeting of his salesmen. How much could they collect without issuing cash receipts? Whatever they could, would make a difference.

At the end of 3 months, a cash amount of 50 lakh was handed over to the General Manager. Franchisees conference was a thumping success with events like Kawwalis, folk dances and a tour of Massorie, Haridwar and Rishkesh. Entire 50 lakh cash collected by discreet proforma sale was blown off.

After the conference and extensive picnicking, it was time for hard business. The cycle of credit supplies had to be stopped and Company put back on rails. Cash flow of white money had to be restored but stopping credit supply abruptly would annoy farmer. He must be talked to very gently. Dev geared up for that change: "Thanks Malik for helping us out for 3 months. I guess now you must be in a position for no-credit business."

"Doctor now I need credit all the more. I have expanded my farm to 1 lac capacity. Now I need credit all the more."

"Company at the moment is cash squeezed and not in a position to extend credit."

"That's unfair Doctor. When it suites you, credit is good. When it doesn't, it's bad. This is not business."

"Malik try to understand my problem. We are not a Govt. Department with unlimited resources. I will give you credit for one month more. Our chicks are of world class quality and quality demands price."

"This old argument doesn't hold water, Doctor. Many new Hatcheries have come up. Their chicks are as good as yours and in addition they are available on huge credit. Your ex-employee Rajinder Singh has already given me a business proposal."

"So you will switch to another breeder?"

"Yes, if you don't increase my credit limit to 50 thousand chicks. Rajinder is ready to supply me 50 thousand chicks on 2 months' credit. What say?'

"Rajinder is selling Skyline, a foreign breed. No one knows how this breed will perform in India. Ours is a tried and tested bird."

Arguments stretched endlessly. One thing was clear. Malik had taken a rigid stand. Rajinder Singh, humiliated and sacked by Doon Hatcheries was out with vengeance. He was poaching ruthlessly on Dev's customer base in Saharanpur.

37

"Is it Dr. Devendra Singh from Ramjilal University?'

"No, Rahul, admission coordinator speaking please."

"But I got this number for Dr. Devender who contacted me for admissions."

"Right. But after field visits, numbers are surrendered to Admission Coordinators. If it is personal then I can give you his changed number."

"It is not personal. I have 10 admissions for B.Tech. How much will I get as commission?

"Rs. 10,000/- per admission."

"I want twenty thousand."

"Sorry, can't give you that much."

"Do you have any training or coaching centers outside of Baghpat?"

"No."

"There is a coaching centre in Yamunanagar which says it is affiliated to Ramjilal University."

"No. No. No. We don't have any such affiliation."

"Who is Sajag Arora?'

"Sajag is our Vice Chairman, son-in-law of the founder Chancellor Mr. Tejram Tomar."

"Well Sajag had personally visited that centre, Navodya Coaching, and said Centre would teach, train and conduct exam but degree/diploma would be awarded by Ramjilal University. I was present in the meeting he conducted."

"To my knowledge there is no such arrangement."

"Can I have a guided tour of University?'

"Yes, any time."

Rahul was a newly recruited admission coordinator. He spoke about the call to senior coordinators, who smiled at him and said, "If someone wants guided tour of University, you should ask: which department? and convey details to Sajag Sir."

"What does it mean?"

"It means you stand chance for a commission of Rs. 10,000/- if all goes well."

"What?"

"Well guided-tour is code word. It means that the person wants to buy a degree. Department means subject. Negotiation is done by Sajag. If deal clinches, you get your commission in cash."

"My God! This is illegal. We can be caught. It will defame University."

"Who will catch us?"

"Crime cell of District Police."

"Police and affiliated all departments are given their share on a regular basis. One who complains about degree would be the first to come under Police baton, for buying a fake degree in the first place."

Rahul came from a poor family. His monthly wages of Rs. 6000/- per month was life line of his family. Ten thousand just for a call was unbelievable. He missed one chance, second he won't.

38

Mukesh scrutinized all AI centers and noted glaring anomalies. Lay Inseminators were operating like Veterinary Doctors, treating sick animals and advising medication. When in-heat animals were presented, AI Center was generally found locked. Farmer was forced to call a private Inseminator as missing a heat meant financial loss. He discussed issue with village Pradhans and called meeting of all Lay Inseminators, numbering 110, at Meerut Milk Plant.

Addressing them in Community Hall, Mukesh lamented that Artificial Insemination result of Meerut zone was going down. Inseminators were not educating farmers about signs of heat, feeding practices and housing norms. They were more interested in treating sick animals which is not their brief.

"Farmers themselves force us to medicate," came a voice from house.

"In that case you should educate farmer on the lines explained to you in your training period."

"Farmer doesn't listen and goes to a private breeder if we stick to rule book. That way we miss out on achieving our AI targets."

"If you can't earn farmer's trust with result oriented service, its better you quit and do something that suits you better."

"What about defective plastic sheaths that you are supplying?'

"Matter came to my notice only yesterday. I have taken it up with Head office."

Plastic sheath is the accessory put on AI gun prior to inseminating the animal. Replace bullet with semen (called straw) and trigger with piston of AI gun; what you have is working model of AI gun. Straw is loaded on the barrel of gun and piston is pushed to deliver semen in female genitalia. Plastic sheath ensures that the semen doesn't go in a wrong direction (backwards). For this, bore of plastic sheath should be in perfect alignment with bore of semen straw. If alignment is lax, semen may be pushed back rather than go forward into damn's uterus as desired. And that was precisely what was happening in field. Semen was seeping back, not going into the female genital tract as intended. Hence alarming fall in conception rate.

Field Vets collected used plastic sheaths which are routinely thrown away after insemination. Examination of sheaths revealed it contained traces of semen. Thus, the semen was being wasted. Hence conception rate dropped ever since the new stock of sheaths was put into use. Who placed order for these plastic sheaths? Senior Vet, Dr. R. K. Singh.

Party who supplied sheaths was new into manufacturing of AI accessories. Why the regular party was sidelined to pick up a new one?

39

All of a sudden Doon Hatcheries was neck deep in trouble. Ishwarchand and Amarjit group actively collaborated with Rajinder Singh, now Sales Manager in Skyline Hatcheries. Saharanpur belt was flush with broiler chicks, all sold on credit by Skyline. This meant that for 2 months Doon hatcheries couldn't sell chicks in Saharanpur belt. Omkumar and Raj Saini, Sales Representatives of Doon Hatcheries, had a sitting with Dev and sought his advice on where to sell.

"Go to Haryana;Panipat , Karnal, Jind and Bhiwani, these are promising markets."

"We can't sell on cash over there. They will ask supplies against promissory note or a postdated bank cheque."

"Don't go to big farmers. Contact small farmers, new entrepreneurs and medium scale chicken traders. They will pay you cash. Within 12 hours of your getting cash, I will ensure dispatch of chicks to your destinations. I will personally look to sales in Dehradun, Kotdwar and Bijnor area."

Downslide in the poultry market was not a new thing. It was a regular phenomenon. But this one was different. Many commercial farmers who reaped gold in bird business, took to Poultry Breeding, and selling day old chicks to reap more gold. Thus, chick producers (Breeders) grew at a faster rate than chick buyers (Commercial Farmers). Production of chicks far exceeded the market demand. Unable to sell, Breeders thought of barter. They had no liquid money to pay for feed/medicine etc. So, they offered chicks as kind-payment towards the purchase of feed/medicine. Dealers in feed and medicine had no option but to accept chicks in place of cash payment to keep the wheel of business moving.

Unsold chicks piled up in Hatcheries. Disease and mortality added to chaos. Many Breeders were advised to shut down operations. Selling of Parent Birds for table led to further fall in the price of table birds (commercial broilers).

Unable to bear sales pressure, Omkumar resigned. The other salesman, Raj Saini resigned soon after. Dev sounded SOS. He was called to Ludhiana Office. What was his suggestion to tide over the crises?

"We should sell our Parent flock to reduce quantum of chick sale. Selling fertilized eggs to Nepal and abroad may also help." Suggested Dev.

"Sale has suddenly gone into shambles. Who should be blamed?'

"Proforma sale on such a big scale was a mistake. We landed ourselves into a credit spin. Then Rajinder Singh came into picture and we lost our market base completely."

"If someone like Rajinder Singh upsets your market, don't you think it shows laxity on your part?'

"Rajinder Singh is on a suicidal path.What he is doing is not business."

"What we are doing is also not business. We have no money to pay salary to our staff. How long will Head Office Pune support us?'

"Poultry industry on the whole is passing through crises."

"Right. And like everyone else, we are also in damage control mode. And our strategy is to close down Doon Hatcheries."

"I see."

"Yes. Staff is being shifted to other units. Your case is tricky. Pune Diagnostic Lab is not willing to take you because of your off beat approach to poultry treatment. And in sales department we have no vacancy. Dr. Dev, under these circumstances there is no way out except that you resign. Dr. Mathur has already resigned on moral grounds."

"I resign right now. Hope I will get this month's salary."

"Don't kid Dev; I will give you 6 month's salary as per the terms of your appointment."

"Thanks a lot."

"God bless you."

40

"Clinical mistakes do happen in Veterinary practice. You should be cautious about diagnosis and never ignore common sense. Remember you are dealing with life. Prudence and patience should be your watch words. Compassion for is life is central to art of healing." Advice came from Dr. B.P Joshi.

A thoroughbred horse died in College Hospital. Suffering from high fever, it was administered Calcium in place of dextrose; horse died instantly. Caesarian in a female canine went well till accidental cut in urinary bladder. Pool of Urine was drained and bladder sutured. But it was too late. Bitch stretched all four legs maximally and went limp, lifeless.

In a string halt operation ligament wasn't cut well. Buffalo continued to drag affected hind leg, unable to bend it on the stifle joint. It was re-operated after a week. Ligament was cut again to free the joint.

A cow was brought to clinic after attempts at her full term delivery failed. Caesarian was immediately carried out and her dead fetus pulled out. Dam survived just for an hour. Brute force used to pull out the fetus, before the caesarian, had caused internal injuries which proved fatal. Caesarian was the only way out, but it was delayed hoping manual pulling will deliver. The delay claimed cow's life.

A cow in ostensible heat (estrous) is inseminated. On day next it discharges a gelatinous bag with black dot, abortion of a month old fetus. Vaginal discharge was mistaken for estrus discharge and inseminating the pregnant dam caused abortion. Cow was not in heat, but in early pregnancy. Mares too exhibit signs of heat in early pregnancy, and allowing stallion to mount causes miscarriage. In reverse case, a non-pregnant bitch may behave like it is pregnant; a condition called fake pregnancy.

Mistakes happen and they have to be paid for. Accountability in medicine has always been a grey area. A Pathologist was asked his opinion on an about-to-die patient. "That's right; now tell me how your knowledge can save the life of this patient." Pathologist had no answer.

Operation was successful but the patient died; sums up predicament of Professional Doctors. Three healing forces work simultaneously for a patient. One, the patient's own living body: two, the attending Doctor: three, the guardians of patient. Aim of all three, ostensibly, is to save the patient. But are these forces mutually compatible?

Bio-system of the patient is first to respond to disease. Pain, fever and other symptoms are a way of the bio-system to cure disease. This is nature-cure view of a disease.

Modern medicine however views these symptoms as ` threat' and tries to suppress them. This goes against the working of bio-system. Medicos act as if bio system has a tendency to score self-goal. Naturopaths laugh, saying nature's wisdom can't be doubted, and nature can't be dictated.

Patient's guardians believe their love and care can make a difference. They believe that money spent on medical care is directly related to their care and compassion for the patient. But the money spent may not necessarily translate into good care. Money spent vibes with sale of medicine, not cure. Symptom suppressing effect of Medicine may please a patient (by fooling mind – body integrity and creating an illusion of cure even as the disease persists). Guardian, and Doctors and the patient may have best of intentions. But, nature, the bio-system, may not be pleased. Rather, it may get infuriated.

This dilemma leaves bio-system to fend for itself all alone in-spite of the other two, or more, perceived helpers. A philosopher rightly remarked: "in spite of Doctor's treatment, patients get cured."

41

Col. K K Verma and his wife Kamala visited their son Vikas in the University Campus, and congratulated him on becoming a father. The bundle of joy, Aashi, united beleaguered families. KK was proud Grandfather now. Did any other promotion in life give him such high? No. Not even the birth of his son Vikas.

Baby had dark skin, like her father and grandfather. Hands and feet active like her grandfather, Col KK, a noted boxer and a marathon runner. His granddaughter would be like him. She would additionally have sharp brain of her father and mother. All the goodness of Verma lineage will flourish in the new born. Col. kissed her forehead.

Father Vikas was on cloud nine. He would never scold her, or set unachievable bench marks for her, as his father did for him. He would love her no end.

Did Col. KK ever love his son Vikas with same intensity as expressed for Aashi? No. Why? When Vikas was born, he was posted in field area; saw baby after 3 months. Ladies in joint family put baby into his arms for a few minutes. That was apt as he really didn't know what to do with the child. He had then tried gobbledygook but felt awkward. How can one talk to a baby? Not Col. Verma's cup of tea. But with Aashi he seemed to talk non-stop. Enticing looks of granddaughter Aashi thrilled him like a school boy: my dear your face is like your mother's, but your hands and feet are ditto mine, so agile, so restless. Aashi, I am your grandfather. My heart missed a beat when your mom was operated. I went to Veshno Devi temple to pray for your health. You seem weak but you have my genes. I was hit in 1971 war. None believed I would survive. But look here I am. You were in ICU and I said you have my genes, you will survive."

Tears trickled in the corner of Col's eyes and he hastily wiped them. He never showed his tears. Now it was difficult to hide them. Baby raised her arm and clutched his cheek. Their eyes met. Expressions on her face changed from curiosity to wonder. Retired Veteran returned to his sweet talk, spontaneous flawless. Vikas and Vinita looked on speechless. Can a child change a senior so radically?

At bed time Col. Verma turned to his wife: "I don't remember talking to baby Vikas like I talked to Aashi today."

"Gents play with babies once in a while, it's a Job cut out for women only."

"How I wish I had loved Vikas more."

42

After Dr. P C Yadav walked out of University, ads were given for the post of Vice Chancellor. None responded. Notoriety of University had spread far and wide. No professional wanted to risk his career by joining Ramjilal. Overly busy in his construction projects, Bhaiyaji couldn't leave University headless. A banker friend of his recommended a Human Resource professional, Sanuj Sharma. He was recruited as OSD (Officer on Special Duty)

Sharma came with a bang. His body language said he will set everything right. A habitual boozer, overweight and motor mouth, he believed in talking and talking. He chatted laughed and joked all the time about how well he executed his foreign assignments and how once he had a brush with Lalu Prasad Yadav of Bihar.

He invited his trusted men for drink, one of them being Narender Tomar, son of Dean Administration Sompal Tomar. In drunken stupor, the two of them poured their heart out to each other.

"What are your career plans Narender?'

"Shift to America."

"What is the delay then?'

"Money. Waiting for it."

"Where from."

"Middlemen who I helped sell fake Certificates."

"Are you not afraid this plan may backfire?'

"It has worked in favor of Prateeksha, Chancellor's elder daughter. She is in South Africa. Akanksha, younger daughter, has moved to Canada. I am about to make it to overseas. There is no future in India."

Sharma was convinced that Ramjilal was a sinking ship. Teaching faculty felt same. Around a shared problem, unity comes easy. If the big wigs of University were engaged in big loot, employees could surely engage in smaller loot. Students gave expensive gifts to their teachers. Examination papers were leaked on payment. Registrar's stamp went missing and a duplicate had to be purchased. Some said that the original stamp was stolen by Sher Singh, Manager Security.

Many visited University in person to get their documents verified. Such visitors were cornered by Sher Singh. He used the stolen 'Registrar Stamp' to verify fake documents as genuine and charged Rs 2000/- for each verification. By the time Management got wind of it and sacked him, he made a couple of lakhs.

43

Mukesh discussed fiasco of Artificial Insemination Project with Preetam Singh, MD Meerut Milk Plant.

A packet of AI sheaths was cut open, one sheath pulled out and mounted on the AI gun. A practical drill was carried out on MD's table and back seepage of semen was proved beyond doubt.

MD was perspiring on forehead. Sheaths were supplied by his brother-in-law sitting in his office.

"What should be done now?" Asked MD looking up to Dr. Mukesh.

"Return entire lot to supplier. Place order with our old supplier for good sheaths."

"Who approved the quality of these sheaths?'

"Dr R K Singh."

"Call him."

Dr. R K Singh said he approved quality only by visual inspection. He was sorry that his mistake proved costly. Sheath Supplier submitted that he would withdraw defective lot and send another lot of good quality sheaths.

"We don't have faith in your sheaths. We can't take risk!" Prajapati's almost shouted.

"Why can't you give him a second chance?" MD flared up.

"He doesn't deserve a second chance! If you want to give him a second chance, please bring another AIO!" Mukesh gave a tit for tat.

"Is this how you talk to your MD?!"

Dr. Mukesh refused to accept anything short of cancellation of Order. MD was bent upon giving a second chance to supplier, his relative.

Word spread that MD was trying to save his relative's business. Board of directors called an urgent meeting. Meeting ended with Mukesh calling shots. MD was charged with dereliction of duty and advised to tender resignation failing which Board would be forced to sack him.

MD agreed to Board's advice and resigned.

44

There was commotion on the main gate of University. Vikas rushed out and saw a group of students hackling some outsiders. Students surged in the direction of Vikas shouting, "Sir they carry fake certificates. These fakes are being verified as genuine by someone in University. They will compete with us for jobs; surely our future is not safe."

"Please cool down. Send these people to OSD office."

Four youths came from Sonepat in Haryana. They had mark sheets for BA program. OSD explained them most politely that their certificates were `fake'. "Who game you these Certificates?"

"We don't know his name. But he sat in this very office, and assured us that Certificates were genuine."

Two youths were in tears. They would lose their job, they said cursing Harender Singh, the middleman who fooled them. They came from poor families. Now they were not only poor but also social out castes. People in their village were cursing them. OSD consoled them and asked if they would like to have tea. No, they said, and left.

Sanuj, Officer on Special duty (OSD) and Vikas sat silently for some time. Sanuj moved head sideways with grim expression on face. Vikas concurred and said: "Sir Things are moving from bad to worse. An email Id Ramjilal@gmail.co.in claims to be official Id of our University and is verifying fake mark sheets as genuine. This is a fake Id. Our University's Id is `Ramjilal@gmail.com."

"Oh God, this should be reported to Cybercrime Cell of the Police department."

"Done already. But fake Id is still operating. I am tired of replying and even shouting on phone that mail from `co.in' is not our communication."

Resentment among regular students of University was justified. Chancellor was informed that students were shouting slogans. He must come and address them. Bhaiyaji arrived the very next day. Facing students in the main hall of University, he said: "There is a conspiracy to defame Ramjilal by some Private Universities who are our competitors. Don't be carried away by rumors. Have faith in management of this University. Nothing illegal is being done here. Today's technology is so advanced that anything can be duplicated and passed as original. University's mark sheets and other Certificates have been copy printed by someone and sold as originals to gullible people. We are not responsible for what they have done. If you find a fake currency note in market, will you blame Government of India for it? If no, then why are you blaming University for fake certificates?"

45

Dev took 15 day's leave for his marriage ceremony. He brought Parul, his newly wed wife to Ludhiana where he served as Veterinary Officer at Punjab Hatcheries. Parul had insisted he leave her at her Parent's house in Delhi. Dev refused outright.

There was something in Parul's behavior which rankled with Dev. It began right from ground zero, their wedding seat in the marriage hall. He offered her a cup of tea which she refused brazenly. Some of his friends saw it and laughed aloud. Dev felt insulted and persisted till she accepted the cup.

On day third of marriage they were sitting before a lady gynecologist. Dev began conversation: "….Penetration is not possible. Wonder if it is due to intact hymen."

Doctor took Parul to adjacent cabin for examination and came out a few minutes later.

"Nothing wrong,' said the lady doctor, "I guess you have some false notion about hymen. It is not a wall like obstruction. See it is something like this…."

Doctor explained with a sketch on paper how hymen was aligned with vaginal wall. Dev shouldn't worry. She is prescribing an ointment for lubrication. After applying ointment, he should try with gentle push.

In their one room apartment in Ludhiana they had a whale of time together. But their vibes were different. Parul had no taste for philosophy, naturopathy or current events. She would fret and fume when Dev didn't return home on time. Dev gave her some books to read to pass time when he was away. She threw them out of the room. Dev collect them under the prying eyes of neighbors. Their bickering was heard by the landlady in adjacent room. She wisely kept matter to herself.

The more Dev tried to understand Parul the more he failed. Parul took strong exception to Dev's eating habits. He explained his pro-health philosophy to her but that was water on duck's back. If he asked something, she wouldn't answer. He would ask for a second time, third and more to get just a cryptic reply. That was immensely irritating. When arguments peaked, Parul would stat wailing and Dev would frantically cajole her lest neighbors hear and rush in.

46

Relieved from his post of Veterinary Officer in Punjab Hatcheries, Dev applied for job at many places, including Ramjilal University. Vinita had informed him that an Assitant Professor for Livestock Production and Management was required in the University. He was interviewed by Chancellor Tejram. First question asked was: "why did you resign from Punjab Hatcheries?'

"For better future prospects."

"At the age of 50 you are searching better prospects. This is age for settlement and not job shifting."

"My daughter is married and settled in her career. I am a free man."

"One child family- good! Is your wife working? We believe in hiring couples."

"No. She is house wife and we are not living together for the past 10 years."

"Divorced?'

"Not divorced. Living separately without divorce."

"Any way. We will give you one administrative assignment in addition to your teaching job?'

"No problem."

"When can you join?'

"Tomorrow."

"Please do."

Vikas and Vinita were overjoyed. Dev, a family member, was joining them. Dev was assigned additional charge of Deputy Registrar. Vikas continued to function as Assistant Registrar.

In his first lecture for 1st year of BSc-Agriculture program, Dev began by asking how many students came from rural background. Just about one fourth. High heeled, Jeans clad bob cut girls were part of program. Did they tend to an animal, a cow or a buffalo? Only a few did. Some did attend to pet dogs.

47

Having known ins and outs of University, Sanuj was keen to make some quick bucks. Construction work is best for spending less and showing more and pocketing the difference. A Thousand admissions were expected from Scholarship quota of Bihar and Jharkhand. Existing space in Hostel would be insufficient, argued Sanuj with Bhaiyaji. His construction plan for adding more rooms to existing Hostel was approved.

Bhaiyaji had his own spies in campus who read into OSD's plan and informed him on phone. Construction work was stopped mid-way.

Hostel Mess was another area that could pay off. Mess is perennial whipping boy for hostellers. For any grievance, food becomes the reason. It is not tasty, chapattis are hard, scheduled menu hasn't been followed, so on and so forth. Vikas had investigated many cases of clash between mess manager and the students. He consistently reported that food in mess was reasonably good. Better arrangement wasn't possible in the budget sanctioned by University. Students were merely venting their ire on food. When last date for paying fee wasn't extended, students complained of daal being watery and rice stale. When a rowdy was caught cheating in exam he instigated students to boycott dinner on the ground that a cook in the mess was misbehaving. Students detained from sitting in examination for insufficient attendance quarreled with Mess Manager for no rhyme or reason. If two rival student groups had some issue, the best place to settle it was dining table.

Sanuj understood this mess-syndrome and became Judge Jury and executioner to Mess Brawls. Incumbent Mess Contractor was fired for poor quality of food and a new Contractor was brought in. Rate fixed was Rs. 80/- per meal for a consumer base of 250. If hostellers were less than this number, bill will be raised for 250 only. If number exceeded 250 then bill be raised at the rate of Rs 70/- per meal.

New arrangement worked well for a month but the number of hostel students didn't rise to the threshold 250. Most of new admissions preferred hiring rooms in Baghpat Township saying that hostel fee was high. Bhaiyaji passed Mess bill for 250 against 150 actual consumers for some time, but finally gave up. Why should he pay for 250 when only 150 ate in Mess?

Mess Contractor flared up. Student number was none of his faults. He will not accept cut in payment. He will go to court. University indeed had no right to cut payment, observed Dev. If case went to court, University would lose. Accordingly he dialed to Bhaiyaji that Contractor had to be paid for a minimum of 250 consumers per day. If hostellers were less than anticipated at the time of signing mess contract, OSD is answerable, not the Mess Contractor.

Tejram deputed a local mediator for out- of- court settlement of mess issue. In a week's time, matter was sorted out. Mess was given to another Contractor arranged by Bhaiyaji from Meerut.

Sanuj was asked to resign.

48

"My name is Brigadier Sugriv Singh. My friends call me Sugriv Singh Ramayanwala. I am your new VC, thanks to Chancellor Tejramji, who is my relative. His wife and my wife are cousin sisters.

Bhaiyaji smiled from ear to ear as the new incumbent introduced himself in University's Conference hall. Sugriv continued: "I was a free bird after my retirement but became diabetic and overweight. Someone suggested to me that I should visit Baba Amarnath Ashram at Haridwar. I went there, learned Yoga and meditation and cured myself. Impressed with Ashram's holistic life style, I joined Baba's Vidyapeeth as Honorary Vice Chancellor. Government of India pays me a lakh of rupees per month as pension, so I refused even a token salary that Baba offered me. I did regular Yoga, taught Management and English language to students and lived like a Sanyasi (recluse). My wife though objected to my life as a brahamchari (celibate)......."

There was laughter in house.

"........So she conspired with her sister to bring me to this University. She said Ramjilal University was in rough waters and that only I could bail it out. Tejram personally called me on phone to say VC's chair was vacant and that I must take it."

Brigadier said he was happy at Amarnath Vidyapeeth, living like a hermit, but he believed more in living for the society than living for the self. Someone advised Swamy Dayanand to go to Himalyas and concentrate on his own salvation rather than reform society and endanger his life. Swami Ji replied, "I will keep working for society even if my enemies turn my fingers into wicks and burn them."

"I come here with the same reformist zeal of Swamy Dayanand. When I knew that this University is being defamed by someone operating a fake degree racket, I resolved to come out of my self-imposed Sanyas and do something for society. My father-in-law was a renowned teacher who taught me Mathematic in school. He always inspired me to do something for the society. My joining here is my way of paying tribute to my late father-in-law. I am here to clean this temple of learning and I need cooperation of you all."

Meeting ended with resounding claps.

49

Dev had to go for a 5 days' training in Diagnostic Techniques to Pune. When he returned he found Parul giving him hard looks. He got irritated. Was that the way to welcome a husband home? Dev tried to keep his cool. Parul remained aloof and refused to talk. Dev was used to her tantrums, but this time it was unbearable.

"What's wrong with you?! What has happened! Has someone misbehaved with you?! He shouted.

That made Parul break into tears and cry. Dev covered her mouth: what are you doing, neighbors will hear. But Parul was unstoppable. When she finally calmed down she revealed that Dr.Sudhir Patil visited her in Dev's absence to enquire about her welfare and put his hand on her shoulder. He smelled of alcohol. She was shocked by his behavior and shoved his hand away. He told her, "Can I help you in any way? Since Dev Sahb is away, if you have any problem at any time, please call for me." She was stunned and didn't know how to react. Mrs. Patil and she were friends and frequently called on each other.

Sudhir's weakness for wine and women was well known. Mrs. Patil contemplated divorcing him on more than one occasion. There were stories galore of how bitterly they quarreled and then patched up in the interest of their growing son.

"I will meet Patil tomorrow and take him to task." Dev assured Parul.

"No don't do that."

"Why?"

"Actually Mrs. Patil and I are good friend. She herself told me that her husband is wayward and that I should be careful if he calls on me any time."

"OK, I will bring Dr. Patil before you and force him to apologize for his misbehavior."

"Don't do that. I will talk to Bhabiji myself. I don't want this matter to become public."

50

Brig. Sugriv loved mingling with students and know their problems. Students became his eyes and ears and he acted swiftly on inputs received from them. Three teachers were given marching orders. One took money to cover up shortage of attendance, another to reveal questions set in the examination paper. Third teacher wanted friendship with a B.Tech girl. "I am already your friend on face book sir", she laughed. "That's right, but I want a different kind of friendship", said teacher. Girl went straight to VC, and teacher was forced to resign.

Those who came for verification of fake certificates were now routed through VC's office. One of them was asked: "who gave you these certificates?'

"Bhanu."

"Call Bhanu!' shouted VC on intercom.

As Bhanu walked into VC's office,the visitor recognized him. Yes he is the man. Bhanu understood the matter and said marksheets in question were given by him under directions from Bhaiyaji the Chancellor. Brig. immediately rang up to Chancellor for confirmation. Bhanu is lying, said Bhaiyaji. Bhanu broke into tears. "Why would I tell a lie? These were given to me by Vinod Sharma of marketing team. He said Bhaiyaji wanted it delivered on given address."

Dr. Dev was called in. Dev was disturbed by props of 'Bhaiya Ji wants it' since pretty long. Every tom dick and harry said 'Bhaiyaji wants it'. You can't ring to Chancellor every time and ask, "sir are these your orders?"

Brig. Sugriv apprised Bhaiyaji that too many people were quoting him. Was that correct? Not correct, replied Bhaiyaji, "I don't talk to lower cadre. If I have to say something I say it only and only through VC's office."

VC turned to visitor. "I am sorry I can't help you. These Certificates are fake. I am sure you jolly well knew it when you paid someone for these documents. Be sure University has nothing to do with it. We are trying to go to the bottom of problem. Now you can go."

51

Col. Verma was a changed man. He remembered his late father often and regretted acrimony with him. Father and son may have differences but ought to remain on talking terms. He should have at least attended father's last rites.

"Why did you carry so much of venom against your father?' Asked his wife Kamala, playing with baby Aashi in her lap.

"I guess my angst against dad began when as a school boy I saw him hit my mother. She was working in kitchen. He picked up a burning wood and hit her on back. Mother ran from kitchen into adjacent room and latched door from inside. Father kept banging outside but she didn't open it. The picture remains etched in my memory like it happened yesterday. But now I realize my father was a victim of circumstances. He did so much for me. And all I remember of him is battery of my mother. How stupid of me!"

"He worked tirelessly for the family. He risked his life by joining army in 2nd world war, started a Dairy Farm in Delhi to supplement agricultural income." Added Kamla

"Yes. Once I had intense ear ache. He cajoled me in his lap all through the night. In the morning he unleashed bullocks, picked up his plough and walked out for agriculture work. Mother prevailed on him to take rest as he had been awake all night, but he ignored her."

"You have changed so much after your heart attack. And birth of Aashi has changed you all the more."

"You are right. I saw death very close to me while I was in ICU. A team of Doctors struggled all night to revive me. And I had strange dreams. My father coming live and saying: don't worry, you will be alright."

"He was so fond of Vikas. Always carried him along whenever he went to fairs and wrestling matches. Ever since we left village, Vikas missed his grandfather and often wept remembering him."

"Kamla you should have checked me when I decided to break from joint family. You could have done that."

"I thought we were moving toward better environment for our son."

"Family, extended family, is the environment that really counts. We denied this to our son. I took him to coaching center, Psychologists and even my colleagues for counseling. Yet he remained problematic in his school and college days. Had I taken him to his grandfather, it would have done him lot good."

"It's strange that we should choose a way that leads to disaster. Vikas was doing so well in Hindi medium school. Switching to English medium bogged him down."

"I wonder if it was my commando training that made me insensitive to relationships. We were taught to be cruel to enemy. But cruelty became part of my behavior. I used to slap Vikas so badly, even as I hated my own father for beating my mother. I have decided to go to village, seek forgiveness for ignoring my father and transfer all my land in the name of my step brother. Vikas and Vinita will also go with me."

"I will request Vinita's parents too to accompany us. Indeed, birth of Aashi has brought unity and happiness for family."

"Now I can die in piece."

"Don't talk of death. For us life has just begun, and you talk of death. Let's live fulsome first."

52

"Dev you resigned from job and didn't inform me." It was Harichand Purohit from Meerut.

"Sorry papa. But I have joined Ramjilal University at Baghpat. I will be with you on all week ends now."

"No need to do any job now. We need you at home."

"I am coming to you this week end. Then we will discuss."

Hari was leading a blissful retired life. A teacher by nature as well as vocation, he was awarded President's Gold Medal for his outstanding contribution to the field of education. His wife Vidya was home maker.

All was well with Purohit family till marriage of their only son, Dev. Parul's father Jagdish and Hari were class fellows in their Secondary education. A common friend brought the 2 families together for matrimonial alliance.

Dev had gone alone to see Parul at their Delhi residence. Jagdish, clad in Kurta-pajama, welcomed him. They sat chatting for half an hour when sensing Dev's unease he called out: Parul! Her mother said she was getting ready. Finally Parul came, along with her younger sister and two younger brothers. Parul was 5th proposal for Dev. Earlier 4 generated lot of heat. He didn't know how to say 'no' and ended up slighting girl's family. Lot of sensitivity is attached to the meeting of the boy and the girl. Dev wasn't mature enough for such social matters but Hari thought Dev must be in forefront as it was a matter of Dev's life. Parents are there with their blessings, but decision should be taken by the boy and the girl, Hari was fond of saying.

Parul came in carrying glasses of water on a tray and thrust a glass in Dev's Direction. Dev, already overload with cold drinks by then, took it and forced it down. He could feel his stomach bloat. She sat on a chair adjacent to his. He craned his neck sideways taking care not to look at her face directly and appear uncivil. His gaze stayed for some time on her belly and neck. Then, taking a deep breath he looked up in her eyes and ask: would you like to pursue higher studies? She answered in negative. Parul told him later she felt uncomfortable with his gaze when he went to see her.

53

It was foundation day of Ramjilal University. Brig. Sugriv Singh was dot on time. Stage was ready but hardly 50 students were there in audience. Worried Vikas apologized to VC. Staff has been deputed to gather students, he said. They will all be here in 10 minutes.

"Don't worry. Start the program. If students have no attachment with their University, so be it." Observed VC and directed the Anchor on stage to get going.

As the event progressed, students poured in and the hall was packed to full. In an hour's time program concluded. Note of Thanks was given by Dr. Dev Purohit. He regretted students' late arrival for program and hoped students would behave in future. Celebrations over, VC called for a meeting in his office. "Where is Dean Administration Mr.Sompal Tomar?" he asked.

"Sir he comes here once in a while. Generally works in Meerut Office and looks to University's legal cases."

"This is not acceptable to me."

Name of Sompal Tomar was removed from University roster. This was resented by Chancellor. But VC remained firm. Let Tomar be an employee of Tej Ram's Construction Company at Meerut. "My Dean Administration now onwards is Dr. Dev Purohit. His charge of Deputy Registrar will go to Vikas Verma. If you don't approve of this then please accept my resignation." Thundered VC like an Army Commander.

Straight talk of VC unnerved Tejram. But there was no way out. University was getting summons from court. Commissioner RTI was breathing on his neck. PF department had black listed University for not providing Provident Fund cover to employees. Some students had also filed case against University. After few days of admission to University they realized they were at a wrong place. They wanted their fee back which was refused, so they went to court. Brig. Sugriv was indispensable. A Headless University in this hour of crises would be catastrophic.

In the evening VC went for a walk and inspected the University's Dairy unit. He wanted to see feed store. A quintal of Cottonseed Cake was received a day before. "Where is it stored?" asked VC. The Dairy Manager, Sis Pal, had no answer.

"See me in my office tomorrow,' said VC.

54

Leaving hostel mess at Mathura abruptly and jumping into non-conventional eating was hard but it had to be done. If you toy with an idea, the idea can toy with you in same measure. Mind is a horse. You can train it up to a point. Beyond that it has to be unleashed. Dev, in third year of his B.V.Sc& A.H program, finally took the plunge. He roasted a handful of wheat grains on hot plate. Sprinkled salt over it and ate with raw groundnut and onion. Wheat grains must con his bio-system into believing that chapatti/roti was still a part of his diet. Onion was his weakness since childhood.

Reasons for choosing raw groundnut were technical. It was high protein and high energy food. Secondly, groundnut oil was prescribed for stomach gas in domestic animals. Thirdly it was cheap and easy to consume as-such.

Major turnaround in staple food was a rocking experience. Dev sat alert and attentive for his afternoon class while his other colleagues felt drowsy after sumptuous lunch. "Wake up!" Teachers threw chalk on sleepy ones to alert them of what was being taught in class room.

Dev noticed major change in his sleeping pattern. He hit bed at 5 Pm in evening and got up at 1 a.m. Prepared tea and studied till 3a.m., then again went to sleep. Second wakeup was naturally delayed and he would run for class with hurried face wash. At times he didn't return to his room for lunch. Sweets, snacks and tea at canteen made his lunch. Dinner was flush with milk supplied from College Dairy Farm at subsidized rate.

Dev lost weight. He gorged on tea, biscuits and fruits. One of his seniors took liquor. Could he do the same? Sometimes he felt low on energy. Let him begin with beer. He procured a bottle. It was too bitter to drink. He threw away the bottle. Alcohol didn't suit him.

Tea became his crutch. His dreams while asleep were as weird as his sleeping times. He dreamt some strong force pulling him into skies above. He caught hold of bed tightly and shouted to be saved. Then he woke up, heart beating fast. He repeatedly had such dreams which invariably disturbed his sleep.

What did those dreams indicate? Would he be going in a direction he didn't want to go? In some dreams he saw himself running with high jumps. His descent from jumps was like a feather and he enjoyed the touch down. But being pulled up fast by skies above terrified him no end.

55

Sis Pal, the Dairy Manager, reported to VC at 10 a.m. Dev was already there. VC turned to Dev and asked, "Can 10 heads of cattle, 5 of them dry, eat a quintals of cottonseed cake in 3 days?"

"No way," said Dev, "I see all the animals grazing on lush green grass all day. That can sustain up to 10 Kg of milk per animal without any concentrate."

"What do you say Sis Pal?"

"I am sorry sir. I have to marry my daughter next month."

"So you will marry your daughter by cheating this University."

"Chancellor is my maternal uncle. He knows my problem. That's why he gave me this Job."

"Did he tell you to earn money by cheating this University?"

Dev at this point sought to intervene, asking Sis Pal to leave the office. Turning to VC he said: "Sir, indeed he has been asked to earn money by cheating this University."

"Dev are you in your senses?"

"Sir our Bhaiyaji gives job to his relatives and allows them loot. That is his way of obliging them and managing this University."

"Are you crazy, Dev?"

"Not at all. Cross check with our Lawyer Vinesh Sharma if you don't believe me."

"Do you want me to believe that Tejram wants his employees to loot this University?"

"Not all. Only selected and favored employees are given this privilege."

"What can he gain by such approach?"

"He gets muddied water in which he can fish, fire someone he wants, and humiliate top management. Have you heard the case of Sher Singh, the security manager?"

"Yes he had stolen Registrar's Official stamp and was verifying documents clandestinely. He was sacked for this."

"This is not the entire story. Sher Singh broke down during Police interrogation and revealed that he had blessing of Bhaiyaji in doing what he did."

VC laughed loud. Never heard of such management in my life time, Oh God, he said gaining his composure.

"Ok, if Bhaiya Ji has a way of working, Sugriv too has one. I want thorough investigation of where 1 quintal of cattle feed has gone. Payment of this consignment should be stopped. Check all loose points in security set up. Sis Ram must be suspended with immediate effect and Dairy should be handed over to someone else. If possible, take a confessional statement from Sis Ram. And I would like to meet Advocate Vinesh Sharma tomorrow."

56

Sacking of MD Meerut Milk Union, Preetam Singh, came as a rude shock to lobby that grew and flourished under him. New MD, Rajesh Mittal was protégé of Preetam Singh. First thing Mittal did after taking over charge at Meerut Union was to call Mukesh and discuss matters.

"Dr. Mukesh I have gone through your personal file and I find you jump on to writing without due diligence. Shooting out memos every now and then is not good for departmental integrity."

"Are you advising me or warning me?"

"Please don't misunderstand; I just want to know you better."

"Then let me correct you sir, I write only as last resort."

"In case of Mohan Lal, driver, you were impulsive."

"No I was not. I warned him thrice to behave. Instead of relenting, he challenged me to write to MD. I did that and he was suspended."

"You must know that drivers are lowly educated people with rough manners. To them you must appear as guardian, not boss."

"Don't guardians punish their wards?"

"Yes they do. But why should you recommended his reinstatement on the very next day?"

"Because he fell at my feet and wept."

"That is poor management. If you relented on his pleading, it only shows charge against him was not substantive. Instead of suspension if you had called for his explanation that would have been a better action on your part."

"Well I may not be knowing nuances of management. But Mohan Lal got what he deserved. He never misbehaved with any other staff in future."

Mittal called for tea and requested Mukesh to relax. He wanted him to know that there was more to suspension of Mohan Lal than just the memo he shot against him. Real story was that it was someone else who wanted Mohanlal sacked. Mukesh's action came as blessing for him as then he would recruit one of his relatives as driver in place of Mohanlal. Revoking his suspension was a dampener for that someone and he blamed MD Preetam Singh for accepting your advice for the same. That someone settled score by sacking Preetam Singh in a development related to AI plastic sheaths. Otherwise Preetam could well have been pardoned than sacked.

Dr. Mukesh heard him patiently and submitted that he had no knowledge of behind the scene activities. He only did his duty. For every action there is bound to be some fall out. Little can be done to check a fall out.

"We surely can do something about it," said Mittal, "by behaving as professional brothers. We all commit mistakes which we can either blow up or course correct. If we fight among ourselves, we suffer and image of department takes a beating. Perhaps you are not aware, Preetam Singh was a dedicated professional. We lost him because you crossed sword with him."

"Well, I am sorry if inadvertently I have harmed someone. My focus is on my work alone."

"Your focus should be on your family also. You have a growing daughter."

"Why drag my daughter into it?!'

"Don't take me wrong. She is my daughter too."

57

Vinesh Sharma, Consultant Advocate, paid weekly visits to University. Generally he whiled away time in loose talks and attended to legal matters only when he was done with frolics. This was his first meeting with Brig. Sugriv Singh.

VC perused some legal files and was not happy the way things were moving. Sharma said Chancellor interfered in his work. In Dahia Constructions case he hired a senior advocate for 30,000/- Rupees with Chancellor's permission. But till date promised fee has not been released.

"Should I talk to Tejram about this payment?"

"Please do. That advocate is cursing me day in and day out."

Brig. Sugriv called Bhaiyaji on his cell phone and walked out of office for talking. He came back after 10 minutes.

"OK Sharmaji, for the moment you prepare to go to Yamunanagar. You have a date in consumer court this week. On your return we will have a sitting."

As Vinesh left office, VC called for Vikas Verma. Verma came in and took seat.

"Is it true Vermaji that Vinesh swindled Rs. 30000/- from University?"

"Yes. He was sent to Education Department, Lucknow for some work. On return he submitted bills one of which was a hand written note saying he paid Rs.30, 000/- to Director Education as bribe. Sharma was authorized to bribe government officials if that helped cause of University in some way. So the money was reimbursed to him. Unfortunately Director in question turned out to be a distant relative of Chancellor and met him in a social function. Talk of Rs 30,000/- surfaced in their talk and a visibly insulted Director said he never took any bribe. Bhaiyaji apologized. Deceit on part of Vinesh was proved beyond doubt. Enraged Bhaiyaji directed Vinesh to return Rs. 30,000/- to University. Vinesh refused outright and said Director Education was double crossing them."

Now it was time to call Dev Purohit.

"Dr. Purohit I am confused about who to believe and who not to." Said a visibly strained Brig. Sugriv.

"Same here Sir. Everything appears jumbled up. My teaching time is spent well. But as Dean Administration, I get confused and depressed."

"What happened to Sis Ram case?'

"Sis Ram is hand in glove with feed supplier. Fake bill was raised, feed was never delivered. Security man who made fake entry in gate pass has been sacked."

"And what about non-payment of electricity bill by PNB for their ATM in University campus?

"Bill is regularly paid to PNB. But that money is pocketed by our Accountant every month."

"What is this nonsense?"

"This is as per Chancellor's will. Every single paisa of cash flow is monitored from Meerut. This is one of the transactions which are never shown in account books."

58

After boy-meet-girl ritual with Parul, Dev returned home and said to his parents: "girl is OK." He then returned to duty at Ludhiana.

There was silence for a week and Dev Grew impatient. He wrote to his father enquiring about progress in matrimony. Father replied that Parul's family was hesitant to proceed in the matter. They felt Dev, as Veterinary Doctor, would be posted in villages and that Parul would find it difficult to live in villages.

In an earlier negotiation for Dev, his father, Harichand had covertly hinted to dowry and the parents of girl had backed out. Dev had tried damage control but failed. Fearing a repeat, he wrote directly to Parul's father seeking categorical answer. Very next day he received a letter from his father Hari saying "they have given a categorical No." Immediately Dev wrote a second letter to Parul's father. "Please ignore the letter I wrote to you yesterday. My father writes to me that you are not interested in me. So Parul's photograph is being returned herewith."

Matter seemed closed till a letter arrived from Jagdish, Parul's father. It said he never said 'no' to alliance. He had only asked for a week's time to consult his elder brother who lived in a Meerut village. On first visit brother was not available. On second visit his brother met him and gave his go ahead. "I, through this letter, again confirm 'yes' from our side. Engagement will be in October and marriage in December."

In the mean while Harichand had gone to see another match for Dev. "Enough of match hunting," Dev wrote to his father, "Somewhere we have to put an end to this exercise. Let us rest this case with Parul."

In the process of long drawn matrimonial search, Dev earned ire of one senior colleague who sent him a marriage proposal. When Dev rejected it, the senior was upset. "Why didn't you return girl's photograph?" Senior asked in an angrily worded letter. Photo was misplaced and couldn't be found. An army officer's daughter didn't go well because of her father's wrong input. Father said his daughter appeared for bank exam. First question Dev asked was "how were you bank exams?" Girl said she gave no exam. A Dairy farmer's daughter was side lined because of low education.

Fed up of too many negotiations, Dev wanted to move on. He settled for Parul.

59

A request for re-evaluation of answer sheet was received. Student attempted all questions and hoped to get 80% marks. What he actually got was zero.

Investigation revealed that the examiner, by oversight, forgot to check one answer sheet. Unchecked copy got submitted along with the checked lot for the posting of marks-scored. Unchecked copy should have been returned to examiner by the Controller of Examination (COE) for needful action, but it was not done. COE Pankaj Sharma was called.

"Why did you award zero marks to an unchecked copy?" asked Vikas.

"I didn't do it. Marks are compiled by the dealing clerk."

Dealing clerk Subhash was called and asked the same question. He looked confused and said he might have done it by mistake.

"Mistake! My foot! Even mistake has a base line. 9 may be mistaken for 7. But this answer sheet is absolutely un-checked. How could you take empty space to mean zero?"

Sensing something fishy in the entire matter, Vikas informed Vice Chancellor who called in Dev. Subhash was also called.

Brig. Sugriv looked straight into the eyes of Sibhashand found him cowering with fear. He began softly, "Don't fear me. Treat me as your elder brother. But let me tell you, I will not spare you if you play smart."

"Forgive me Sir. I was forced into it by Pankaj Sir. He got me appointed to this University. I come from a poor family ….."

"Go on I am listening."

"….Sir then I was lured into tweaking score sheet. Border line pass were approached with message that they were failing. They immediately offered money to pass them, and I got my commission."

"In this particular case I told Pankaj to give answer sheet back to teacher but he advised me against it and directed me to show score as zero. He expected student to approach him and negotiate like other students did. But student being topper of his class, he went straight for re-evaluation."

VC punched his intercom,   "Mr. Pankaj can you come over to my office for a minute please?"

60

A Dairy Farm run by Kamdhenu Federation was having multiple problems. Dr. Mukesh was deputed to investigate and submit his report directly to the Chairman.

Mukesh got in touch with the Veterinarian posted at farm and went straight to his office. Vet, Dr. Maha Singh was a diminutive and bespectacled professional frequently quoting from clinical guide book – Merk's Manual. Over a cup of tea he explained what he felt was wrong with the farm. Then the two of them strolled through the animal sheds.

Sheds were poorly ventilated. Sewerage pits were clogged and drainage defective. Hose pipes for cleaning the floor were unkempt. Cool air stabbed in through loosely hung plastic curtains. Solar heaters on roof tops were dysfunctional. Mukesh frowned: "What is this Doctor?'

"Sir this is the job of Farm Manager."

"And your job is to wait till an animal falls ill and then you jab it with antibiotics, am I right?"

"But Sir my job is to treat."

"Disease prevention is also your job. You know a sick buildings is a threat to livestock health. Call Farm Manager, I will speak to him."

Farm Manager Virender lamented that labor was defiant. "If I take them to task they run to this or that director and I am forced to tolerate them."

"What else?"

"I suspect quality of cattle feed. But we are forced to buy feed from Federation's in-house Feed Mill."

"What is your take on cattle feed Dr. Maha Singh?"

"It's not up to the mark. I have written several letters to the Nutritionist posted at Feed Mill. He says he tests every batch of feed for Energy, Protein and Mineral contents. Feed is released to Farms only when all parameters are in prescribed limits."

"I am not a Doctor," said Virender, "but I know that taste of pudding lies in eating it. I know for sure that my animals are not happy eating this feed."

"OK Virender I authorize you to buy a different brand of Cattle feed from open market. Don't feed in-house brand for the next 24 hours. Thereafter I will see how it impacts Milk yield."

Virender did as directed. Hike in milk yield was a significant 15%. Mukesh dialed to Chairman that he wanted feed from open market and not from their in-house unit. Labor problem was also highlighted. On the lines of report submitted, Special Investigation Committee was formed to look into the issues raised by Dr. Mukesh.

61

The very next day of his marriage, first thing that Dev noticed was touch-me-not demeanor of Parul. Given to bouts of whining and sulking, she lived in a world of her own. She broke out of a conversation abruptly, with brazen indifference. He ignored her trespasses thinking she was a newly wedded bride and needed time to adjust to change. His parents though were hurt with cryptic answers and indifference of their newly arrived daughter-in-law.

On their first night together her first submission was as blunt as it could be. She said: "for first 3 years I don't want a baby and we will have only one baby be it a boy or a girl." Even though Dev thought on similar line, her manner of saying was awkward. He kept a cool exterior but on the inside he felt hit in the stomach. To her blabber, "leave me in Delhi now and bring me back after 2 months," he gave a straight 'no'. Parul gave angry looks but Dev held his ground and brought her along with him to Ludhiana.

At Ludhiana, Parul looked scornfully at the one room apartment Dev lived in with just two folding beds. Her father had given a double bed, an Almara and a big trunk as marriage gifts, but these were left behind with Dev's parents. Kitchen had Kerosene stove; no LPG gas. She had difficulty burning the stove and every time Dev had to chip in for help.

"You haven't eaten for the past 4 days." Remarked Parul rather astonished as Dev returned from office one day.

"Didn't I have tea, milk, and the vegetables that you cooked?'

"You haven't taken a single chapatti."

"That's how I eat, mostly fruits and raw vegetables."

"Do you suffer from some disease? Why can't you eat like other normal people?"

"Are you crazy? Instead of feeling happy that I reduce your kitchen work load, you are cursing me."

"Reducing my kitchen work? My foot! It takes same labor and cost to cook for 2 as for one. At least for sake of company you should eat with me."

"I can't. I don't eat with time. I eat only and only when I am hungry. My eating is several times in a day in small lots. It is more like snacking all the time."

Parul was good at cooking; good only at cooking rather. And there was Dev, professing that cooking was mother of all ills. Biblical story of forbidden apple is metaphorical, he said. His take on the story was different. It wasn't some mysterious apple that God forbade Adam and Eve to eat. God in fact directed them never to cook their food, but live on raw and natural diet. Adam and Eve lived happily in heaven as long as they ate raw, and ate only when hungry. Accidental access to cooked food fired their taste buds and they started eating for pleasure-of-eating. This infuriated God and He rusticated Adam and Eve from heaven. They were dropped on earth to spend major part of their life searching food, cooking food, eating and drinking; an existence shorn of bliss.

62

Vinita invited Dev for dinner and asked him how he felt switching to job in University. All-is-well, said Dev imitating a filmy dialogue and adding, but all is not well. A day before, Bhaiyaji was summoned by High Court of Karnataka. There he deposed that he as head of institution can't be blamed for what his employees may have done. All he could do and did do was to expel any one he suspected of involvement in any wrong doing.

"So Court absolved him of charges?" asked Vinita.

"No way. He has a long way to go and face a lot. This is just the beginning."

"I got a call from CID Inspector Hema Ram" said Vikas. "He told me that bank accounts of Sajag Arora and his father have been sealed. Their laptops and cell phones have also been confiscated and trail of their communications is being perused. Their passports too have been confiscated."

"Chancellor is playing smart, but he is badly cornered." Observed Dev.

"His elder son-in-law, Jitender was upset when contacted by Police in connection with fake documents. I understand he has moved court to seek divorce from his wife Prateeksha." Said Vikas.

"Court has granted them separation for six months. After this period they will have to appear before court for the final divorce."

"What is the way now left for Chancellor? In this academic session too, the number of admissions is very low."

"He has introduced a new course, Diploma in Pharmacy with effect from this Academic Session."

"But I see no students."

"You don't see them physically. But on paper they are very much there, full fee paid."

"Really? How do they manage it?"

"Well, there are people in regulatory bodies who can tell you tricks of trade for a consideration. Murlidhar, the new Director, is PhD in Pharmacology. He is a new buddy of Bhaiyaji. In all meetings our Chancellor praises him highly. He repeats time and again: A professional should be like Murlidhar.

"Once upon a time he idolized Col. Jagdeep, the first Registrar of this University. Then Dr. Mahajan, then Dr. Tiwari, the list is endless." Laughed Vikas.

63

"Ideally we shouldn't remove advocate Vinesh Sharma." said VC, "Because he knows too much as an insider and can harm our interests."

"But we have to get rid of him else we will lose many cases that he is fighting for us. We are consulting another lawyer on a regular basis, and Vinesh has come to know of it."   Observed Dev.

"I have called him for a golden handshake today. He is meeting me in afternoon today."

Sharma came with dropped face. Chancellor has consistently abused him, he said. "I remained loyal despite knowing his shady deals. People close to him are stabbing him in the back. And he is venting his anger on me, me, who consistently stood for him."

"I understand Sharma," said Brig. Sugriv, "but I have to proceed with realities presented to me. Our new lawyer has indicated many a lapses in your presentations and we have no option other than to say good bye to you."

"OK, give me 3 month's salary and I will quit."

"I will give you this amount. But I am keen to know your side of the story of fake certificates."

"This I can reveal only in private."

VC requested Dev to leave office.

"Ok, now only two of us are here."

"No, there are CCTV cameras above in this office, let us go out for a stroll in University campus."

Vinesh began his story as the two of them walked out of the main building in University Campus. Vinesh said that from the very beginning he saw a mismatch between what Bhaiyaji said and what he meant to say and do. "I thought my being a lawyer kept him from being candid before me. To make him comfortable I opened my cards and said I can earn in number 2 and give him every month, all that Bhaiyaji had to do was to tell me how much money he wanted. This, to my surprise, made him all the more skeptical of me. Our situation was like two men sleeping with a woman and each believing he alone had right to fuck her; the other should just enjoy deep sleep. How is that possible? I laugh when he sermonizes in a meeting. That's like a devil quoting scriptures."

"I heard from some sources that Chancellor is a Womanizer."

"Very right. Go on the top floor of University Building. You will find a big room with attached bath; almost camouflaged. You will have to look hard to find it. Just look at the interiors of it and you will know what can be the possible utility of that room."

64

If well begun is half done, bad begun is half doom. Dev's marriage didn't begin well. It was destined to break up. But the couple made efforts and pulled it for full 14 years.

During this period Dev got hooked to conventional 3 times eating. Occasionally he fasted, ate fruits and raw vegetables but the baseline had generally shifted to wheat and rice. Actually the shift began even before marriage, when he reported duty at Punjab Hatcheries. On farm visits he was offered drinks. Initially he refused but gradually he accepted. With drinks, eating of conventional cooked food became more frequent, almost regular, and his lean frame filled up.

Within a year of marriage, they were blessed with a daughter. They named her Veena. But their marital life remained as disturbed as before. Dev had visualized himself in the steps of a teacher and his wife as his dutiful disciple. Far from it his life partner had no taste for learning. If arguments stretched, she started crying. "If you want to live peacefully, be a submissive husband," advised his landlord, "that's too little a price for marital peace." Landlord, Mr. Mahesh, was a harassed husband. A teacher of Zoology in a local degree college, his wife taught English language in same college. Couple was issueless. They tried various doctors, treatments, but to no avail. Their infertility, Dr. Dev suggested, was a psychosomatic problem. Mahesh agreed as the couple had a near-divorce situation several times in past. Mrs. Mahesh had a dormant fear of being deserted by her husband. Fear caused her system to reject the developing egg or embryo.

Dev's opinion was well received. Mrs. Mahesh was touched on knowing it from her husband. Suddenly she grew very patronizing of Dev. The tone of her voice oozed immense respect for him.

"Women are very sensitive Dr. Dev, very fragile," said Mr. Mahesh. He was counseling Dev after a rather serious brawl Dev had with Parul and he along with his wife were forced to intervene. "Do you know once my wife refused to go to College for a very petty reason?"

"What?"

"Well, on the previous night I bit her cheek during love making. It was a gentle bite. In the morning she saw a reddish mark there. I saw no such mark. She was visualizing mark on her own, I argued. But she didn't agree and remained closeted at home for the entire day."

65

Pankaj Sharma, Controller of Examination, was suspended and his charge handed over to Vinita.

Cybercrime branch of UP Police came to interrogated him. Pankaj being a Computer Professional was also in-charge of University's official website. He submitted that he operated website only for the first academic year of University i.e. 2008-09. Thereafter it was totally under the control of Meerut Office.

"Who in Meerut office?"

"Many were given contract assignment from time to time. But it was Sajag Arora who guided them all consistently. Sajag's approval was mandatory for all uploads on website. He edited and approved contents, then and then only the website manager accepted them for upload."

"Did you e-mail any content to Sajag for approval?"

"Yes."

"Can I have a print out of that along with reciprocal response from Sajag?'

"Yes I will get it in 5 minutes."

Cops turned to VC Brig. Sugriv. "This is quite a catch. We heard of Sajag Arora from many sources. We quizzed your Chancellor also about him. But we just couldn't nail him. If your Pankaj Sharma gives us print of this particular email, our job is done."

Sharma returned in time, and handed over a couple of stapled print outs. One Cop perused those sheets and his face lit up.

"You have done a good job Pankaj." VC patted his back. "I will recommend your reinstatement on job provided you come clean on certain issues."

"What issues Sir?'

"You meet me tomorrow morning, and then I will tell you."

66

"Papa, can you come over for 3 months? That's your share of Aashi's care. Verma parents have been here for 3 months. Now it is turn of Prajapaties."

It was a call from Vinita. Mukesh agreed and applied for leave. MD was unwilling, maximum that Mukesh was entitled to, was 2 months. Why does he want such a long leave?

"My granddaughter was born premature. My daughter and son-in-law, both are working. Baby needs our care. If you feel there is some administrative hitch, I will resign.

MD informed Chairperson that long holidays for Mukesh will create administrative problems. So it would be better to agree to his resignation and hire a new AIO so that work doesn't suffer.

News of Mukesh leaving Milk Federation spread like wild fire. 'Why' everyone asked. Nothing unusual, Mukesh explained. Not related to my technical report on Kamdhenu Dairy Farm, nor to my brush with ex- MD Preetam Singh. It is a very personal family decision. Some of his well-wishers met him and said, "Dr. Mukesh, please don't hide from us. If someone has pressurized you to resign, please tell us, we will back you to the hilt."

"Rest assured there is no hanky-panky. My farewell is fixed for coming Monday. Do come and wish me well for next inning of my life." Explained Mukesh.

Vinita was delighted to know of her father's resigning from job. Ever since Dev uncle joined University, she had been advising him to resign. Dev uncle would give him a suitable assignment in University. Aashi will now have a regular company of her nana and nani. Who can bring up children better than their own grandparents?

Dev was excited too. His friend Mukesh would be so close to him once again. It would be déjà vu college days. University's

Dairy has to be expended to 100 cows. A vacancy for Project Manager- Dairying is already advertised. Dr. Mukesh would be ideal candidate for it. In addition, Mukesh will also relieve him of teaching job as Dev was deeply involved in administration.

67

With Vinita taking charge of COE (Controller of Examination), many skeletons rolled out from cupboard. Many students declared pass were actually failing when matched with their score in the answer sheets. Such students were presented in VC's office. Students said they paid Pankaj for passing them.

"Yes I took money," reacted Pankaj, "but half of that money I paid to Sompal Tomar. In fact it was Sompal who gave me this idea of making money. Initially I was fearful but he assured me that Chancellor was in know of it and nothing will happen to me."

VC dialed to Chancellor and reported the matter. Chancellor said implicating him was baseless. He agreed though that Pankaj was son of Sompal's close friend and was appointed in University on Sompal's strong recommendation.

"You were quiet for so long Pankaj. How come now you are an honest man?'

"Because, providence has punished me hard. My father, a retired school teacher, died of heart attack yesterday night on knowing about my activities. My wife cried loud that she would prefer to beg in street than live with me."

"O God! You must be home for last rites of your father."

"I have been denied this right too by my younger brothers."

68

Parul habitually got up late in the morning, something that irritated Dev no end. Over the time he learned to adjust to it. Veena, their daughter, was admitted to School in KG class. It was winter morning and she was dressed for school without bath. Dev didn't like it and insisted bath was necessary. Parul said it was too cold for bath. Arguments mounted as clock ticked school time. Dev rushed out with baby and got her seated in school bus waiting outside.

As he returned he couldn't hold himself and said girl would stay in school for 7 hours and would be uncomfortable all because she didn't take her morning bath. Parul was in no mood to relent and that forced Dev to comment on her character and poor education she received at her parent's home. Parul turned table on Dev: "Think of your own dirty family, where even sisters are not spared."

This was clearly a hit below the belt. In an inebriated moment he had revealed to her how as a growing boy he was seduced by his cousin sister.

But Parul wasn't done. "You talk about my character," she said fuming, "think of your own mother's character- deserted by her first husband. Your overage physically handicapped father married her as he was needy. Some even say he bought her for a sum of 50,000/- rupees. And here you are, talking of my character. And what about your own sister, why she lives with her parents and not in-laws."

"You are crossing limit, Parul." Dev warned her.

"I am not. I was ill-treated by your mother in my pregnancy and during delivery. She made faces on knowing that the new born was daughter; she wanted son not daughter."

"I have told you repeatedly not to drag my mother and sister into conversation."

Parul kept shouting and weeping. "My life is ruined,' she cried hysterically, "I better put an end to it." Saying this she reached out to the Kerosene stove, opened it and poured kerosene on her clothes. Dev disengaged her and slapped her hard on head. Next thing he knew was that she was clutching her right year. It was bleeding. Button of Dev's jacket got entangled with her ear ring and pulled it apart. Hearing wails and commotion, Mrs.Mahesh, the land lady rushed in. She picked up the ear ring lying on floor and said: "what have you done Dr. Dev, see her ear is torn and bleeding."

69

Simmi Berwal was hired by Bhaiya Ji with a purpose. He wanted his Pro VC Naresh Mahajan removed and replaced with Dr. Tiwari who Simmi felt would make a good VC. Prof Naresh was doing well as far as academics were concerned. But admissions were poor, student strength was not rising. Slush money earned by fakes was all spent, largely in bribing government officials. Selling of fakes any further was not possible as complaints had gone up to the Prime Minister's office.

Simmi joined as Dean Academics. Right from day one her only job seemed to be to malign Prof. Naresh in some way or the other. When he could not take it any longer, he resigned. Students were shocked. He was the only faculty they found knowledgeable, wise, caring and friendly. His leaving University would be a great loss to students. A group of students contacted him at his residence in University campus. "Nothing unusual," he said, "I have resigned due to some personal issues." But body language of Professor was mismatch. He wiped his eyes discretely, rushed to bathroom and returned to face students after splashing his face with water.

Student group moved to the office of Dean Academics, and requested her to come out in the lawn where students had gathered to hear her version of why Dr. Mahajan resigned. She shouldn't have forwarded his resignation to Bhaiyaji.

"Who am I to forward his resignation? He emailed resignation directly to the Chancellor. This is between him and the Chancellor." Said Simmi in a matter-of-fact way.

Brouhaha died down by day next. Dr. Naresh left University campus with bag and baggage. Within a week's time new incumbent Dr. Badri Nath Tiwari joined as Vice Chancellor.

In his introductory meeting Dr. Tiwari said: "It is my good luck and a blessing from God that I join this institution on the day of Hanuman Jayanti. I would like to compare this University with Construction of a bridge over the sea by Lord Ram. In that gigantic task, a squirrel was seen bringing tiny pieces of wood and trash at the construction site. Seeing this, everyone around started laughing. They advised her to remain away as her contribution was not significant and she could get crushed under someone's foot. Lord Ram overheard it and directed that squirrel be allowed to do her bit. Spirit to contribute, said Ram, was more important than the magnitude of contribution. In the same way I appeal to each one of you: please have the spirit to contribute, and contribute to the building of this University in whatever way possible."

70

PP duo was sitting together after a long gap. Mukesh meanwhile had joined University as Manager Dairy Project. At the same time he was teaching Veterinary Science to B.Sc. Agriculture students.

"Dev I am sorry to ask about your personal life. My knowledge of your marital crises is based on tit bits I have picked up from myriad sources. I also regret having developed a negative opinion about you without cross check. Now I want to make mends for that lapse."

"How?"

"I will go to Bhabiji, your estranged wife Parul, and request her to come back. You two are living separately for the past 10 years."

"She won't come. You will be wasting your time."

"Then why don't you go for legal divorce?"

"Our love for our daughter Veena far outweighs our mutual acrimony. She loves both of us equally and understands why we live separately."

"Every married couple has differences, even overt and covert fights. But a separation lasting so long, that's strange. What triggered this separation?"

"A friend of mine had suggested Parul should, work as Assistant in HR department of his company. That could strike peace in my house as Veena was School going. Parul agreed to proposal. But she could work just for 4 months."

"What happened?'

"She couldn't jell with the staff there. Manager HR, doubting her credentials, sent her mark sheets for verification. Only her high school degree was found to be genuine. Intermediate and Graduation degree was fake."

"O God!"

"Then I had a heated argument with my maternal uncle. He was the person who recommended Parul as match for me. He had known Parul since her birth and was her father's best friend."

"Then your uncle should have taken up the issue with Parul's parents."

"He tried but couldn't."

"Why?'

"Parul's father, far from listening to mamaji, turned tables on him. He accused him of ruining Parul's life by recommending a rogue family. He called my mother a woman of loose character and me a womanizer."

"Did he say anything about Parul's fake educational degree?'

"No. He just called her home and she went there with bag and baggage. Veena was admitted to a Delhi School, and stayed with her mother."

71

"You all are trained Doctors, why then should there be a need to retrain you in diagnostic skills?' Asked Dr. Pitamber Singh, the Chief Instructor at `Animal Care Labs' Pune.

"There is always a scope to learn, and improve on your skills." Said Dev.

"With time microbes keep mutating and causing altered host response. Hence diagnostic skills need constant updating", said another voice from a corner.

"In view of emerging diseases……'

"Well, all of you are right in your own way," said Dr. Singh, "but not realistic. To give you a hint, it is something which is directly affecting our career as practicing Doctors these days."

There was silence in house.

"OK I will give you the answer. But first give me your opinion about quacks or livestock assistants working in Veterinary field."

House was unanimous that quacks are having a field day. Even in poultry field, a good number of consultants are non-vets.

"Why so? Please think hard."

Again there was silence in the house.

"Now listen to me carefully. Animal health care in India is in the hands of 5 gods; not veterinarians. These 5 gods are: Antibiotic, anti-allergic, antipyretic, analgesic and multivitamin. Treatment of any and every disease revolves round these 5 gods. Qualified doctors as well as semi-qualified quacks worship these five gods. What's the difference then between true Doctors and the fake Doctors? Answer is diagnostic practice. Professionals must be diagnostically superior to quacks to keep their good will and practice intact."

Good argument, thought Dev, but not the entire story. Diagnosis does impart some sophistication to clinical practice but that's all about it. Best of Doctors differ in diagnosis. If they agree on diagnosis their line of treatment will differ. Best of tools fail to decipher disease in-time, claims of timely diagnosis notwithstanding. Alternative view on medicine says there are as many diseases as there are patients. But there can't be one doctor for one patient. Patients must be grouped, into diseases. Groups are easier to manage and treat in a commercial set up. One Doctor and his team can address classified patient groups. Treatment is a team work of doctor, pharmacist, nursing homes, patients and their guardians. Their unified action may or may not suit the ultimate interest of patient. But the show must go on.

72

"Dev Uncle Do you think Aunty could be a psychiatric case, something like my own case?' Vikas initiated discussion as Vinita brought tea for the family.

"She could be. I even mooted this idea. But your aunty was quick to react. She said it was I who needed a psychiatrist."

"Really?'

"Yes. She said I don't eat wheat and rice which is staple for most humans. Work like mad for poor wages and get superseded by my subordinates."

"I will meet aunty and tell her my case, if dedicated care has helped me, it will work for her as well."

"From an insider I learned that she had been a loner and difficult child right since childhood. She was a weak in studies. Her father did his best to mainstream her. When she failed in 12th class, her grandparents wanted to take her to village with them. They advised she should discontinue education and get married in farmer's family. Jagdish viewed it a retrograde step and said all his 4 children will do graduation, come what may."

"In our time parents were magnanimous, " said Mukesh Prajapati, "if a child was week in studies, he/she was never forced to go to school."

"In the name of education we are ignoring commonsense. Education is being confused with academics. Our ancestors knew that anything and everything that we do to earn a legitimate living is education." Observed Dev.

It was dinner time and table was ready. All got up and moved to dining room. Dev was surprised to see menu on table. "Wow! What a spread. Salad, juice, roasted grains, lentils. But where is your staple, dal-roti-sabji?'

"Uncle today we decided to eat your way." Smiled Vinita.

"Right!' exclaimed Mrs. and Mr. Mukesh Prajapati.

"Yes uncle." Blinked Vikas.

"Thank you all. But take care; change of diet should be a gradual process. My way was rather blunt and aggressive."

All nodded in agreement.

73

Brig. Sugriv Singh took some moments to recognize him.

"O Col. Balbir Singh! Great to see you! Please come, be seated."

"Ever since you joined this University, I had been trying to meet you. So, how is University?'

"Not good."

"You must be joking. With a man like you on helm University can't go wrong?'

"Indeed it is going in wrong direction. Your younger brother is steering it by remote control."

"No. Munna, I mean Tejram can't do this. I know him since he was born."

Balbir became serious, "Come on Sugriv, tell me what he is doing. I will catch him by the ear if it's something wrong."

"It's a big story. Stay overnight with me. I will tell you everything."

The two army officers slept under one roof and talked till late night. On breakfast table Col Balbir was grim and thoughtful. His younger brother had strayed and he had no idea of how to bring him back. Brig. Sugriv caught his emotion and tried to cheer him up.

"What should be done now?' Asked Balbir taking a sip of tea.

"I suggest we call Tej and counsel him to surrender to investigating agencies. He is still playing smart even as evidence is mounting against him."

"What if he refuses to surrender?'

"In that case both of us will revolt against him and we will begin by calling press conference."

"Agreed."

Brig. Sugriv Singh dialed to Chancellor. There was something extremely urgent that he and his elder brother wanted to discuss with him. He must come soon.

Tejram arrived as requested and remained closeted in VC office till lunch time. Lunch was served in VC's office. Post lunch meeting resumed and ended at 5 PM. Thereafter the three of them went out for a stroll in the University campus.

74

The Republic of India was swept by Modi wave. Clean-India became the buzz word. A declaration on 8th Nov ' 2016: "With effect from tomorrow, all currency notes of 500 and 1000 denominations will no longer remain legal tenders." became the watershed moment in history of independent India. DE-monetization, a forgotten chapter Economics, saw light of the day.

Bhaiyaji was hit hard. He had promised his elder brother to surrender to investigating agencies. He wanted one month's time to brace up for the ordeal. Now another, problem, demonetization stared him in the face. His partners in crime wanted their money back in new currency. Mountains of old 500 and 1000 rupee currency notes that he had in his coffers were now worthless pieces of paper. Harender Singh stood in front of Bhaiyaji. He wanted his money back.

"Please understand my problem." Said Tejram.

"Certificates were bought from you with clear understanding that in case these were deemed fake, you will return my money." Said Harender.

"Anyone who came to me with a note from you got his money. Now the only hard cash with me is what is demonetized."

"That is your problem, not mine. Perhaps you don't know, one of my agents is shot dead. Others are running for their life."

"My assets are before you. Take whatever you want. My car, AC, Watch, gold chain, Generator, whatever you want you can take."

"Give me your car. I will give it to one party that is baying for my blood."

Tej Ram threw away his the keys of his Mercedes car. Harender directed one of his accomplice to drive it to his residence. Tej was worried about cash-load stacked at Sajag's

Gaziabad residence. Sajag at his own level tied up with a banker to exchange defunct currency with new currency.

Tej went to all his poor relatives, doling out wands of banned currency which they could deposit in their bank accounts. All legal channels of converting No 2 into No 1 were exhausted. He didn't want additional problems for his family. So he wanted all illegal cash burnt and destroyed. Sajag was on a different wavelength. He loaded currency notes in his car and went to an agent who promised conversion on commission basis. Currency had to be conveyed at a place near old Delhi Railway station. Sajag's phone was under surveillance of Crime Branch. At destination he was surrounded by cops and arrested.

75

Dev received a call from Economic Offence Wing of Delhi Police.

"Yes I am Dr. Dev Purohit."

"I am ASI Ritesh Yadav. This call is being recorded, so please answer my questions carefully. '

"Yes Sir. Please go ahead."

"There is a posh 2 room set in Delhi's Green Park area in your wife's name. We want to confirm that this is your house."

"No, this is not my house. My wife is living separately from for the past 10 years. I don't know how she managed to buy this house. She is not even working. She is dependent on her father."

"You mean Master Jagdish Purohit?'

"Yes."

"Jagdish is under surveillance for a slew of benami properties. I want to reconfirm that you have not financed any house in your wife's name."

"I confirm that I have not financed any house in my wife's name. I don't have any house even in my own name."

"OK thank you Sir."

"You are welcome."

A few days later Dev got a call from his father-in-law. Why did Dev say that house in Delhi was not his (Dev's)? He (Jagdish) bought the house for him (Dev) and Parul.

"Your daughter deserted me on your call. Since then she hasn't talked to me nor do I have any Knowledge of what she is doing. If you have gifted her house, why are you dragging my name into it?"

"My daughter needed a decent house and I knew you would never be in a position to give her that."

"I have a house in village built by my grandfather. And another in Meerut city in my father's name. I don't need a third house."

"Look Dev, be sensible. Retract the statement you made to Delhi Police. For the past 10 years Parul is shown as senior manager in a private firm owned by my brother-in-law. She is shown drawing a monthly salary of Rs 80,000/- per month."

"I will not retract my statement."

A few days later Jagdish Parihar was arrested and his benami properties confiscated.

76

"Shanti, are you asleep?'

"No, what's the matter?'

"I want to discuss something important." Said Tejram.

"Ok."

"Don't switch on light."

"I thought I will get you tea."

"No need for that. You just listen."

"Hope you are alright. You went for medical checkup. Hope your blood pressure is normal."

"Nothing wrong with my health Shanti, I just want to say that I have betrayed you. Forgive me."

"I don't understand what you are saying."

"Shanti you know my construction business is in the red. But now even University will slip out of my hands."

"But Sugriv Jeejaji told me all is well in University."

"No. tomorrow I will surrender to Police. I may spend rest of my life in jail."

Shanti got up from bed and switched on lights and looked hard at her husband: "you are weeping!'

"Let me weep Shanti. I never showed you my tears, wish I had. I am not so strong and upright as I always pretended. My one daughter will soon become a divorcee. And another's husband is in Police custody, all because of me."

"We are passing through bad time. We will come out of it. Why are you blaming yourself? And why will you go to jail?'

"Because I and Sajag sold fake Certificates, and now we have reached dead end. I am a shame on society. I have kept you in dark. Forgive me Shanti and brace up for future. In my absence, the charge of our 2 daughters would be with you."

"I remember you used to curse corrupt system around you. I always advised you not to pay bribes come what may. We have enough agriculture land to sustain us. Now you tell me that in the process of cursing corruption, you became corrupt yourself."

"I fell into a vicious circle. Money needed to run business outweighed my legitimate earning. We will lose our agriculture land too. It is mortgaged with banks. It would be adjusted against loans that I have taken."

"Still I say don't worry. Our grandparents were agriculture labors. We can restart as labor. Our daughters are educated and serving. I can live with them. We have no liability. Now cheer up. I will get you tea. It is 11PM. We will talk more on issue."

Tejram looked up. Shanti was smiling. He often joked about illiteracy of his wife. With great difficulty she learned to sign in Hindi, for signatures on bank cheques and property documents. But for the moment she seemed to be the wisest person he ever met in his life.

77

Arrest of Sajag was widely discussed in University. Sher Singh, the ex-Security Manager and Amit Sikera, ex-Store Keeper were thoroughly investigated by Crime Branch. There were rumors that summons were sent to the ex-VC Dr. Badri Nath Tiwari as well.

A call was received at CBI office New Delhi. It was from Prateeksha, Tejram's elder daughter. She wanted to talk to Sajag who was there on 15 days' remand. "Sorry madam," said lady at reception, "no calls are allowed for him till his remand period. Desperate Prateeksha rang to her younger sister Akanksha at Ghaziabad.

"Aaki, it's me Prati, Prateeksha from Australia. I am here on an assignment. Please tell me what's wrong at your end. Mummy and Papa's cell phones are in Police custody. Thank God I got your line."

"Didi things are in a mess."

"I know. But what are you doing for damage control."

"Can't do anything Didi. I regret marrying Sajag now. Wish I had heard to your counsel."

"Marriage is always dicey. See Jitendra is divorcing me. I never thought he would do that."

"Sajag lured our father to sell fake degrees. Jitendra shouted at father when he knew about it. You took father's side, provoking Jitendra to divorce you. He thought you too are partner in crime. That way it is Sajag, and not Jitender who is responsible for breaking your marriage."

"But how come you couldn't stop Sajag in his tracks?"

"Didi he said little cheating was part of game. It's only now that I realize what he meant by little. His little was so huge."

"Don't worry Aaki, we have to accept life as it unfolds. Cheer up."

Gossips doing rounds in University Campus were irksome. Brig. Sugriv therefore called for a meeting of students and teachers. In the meeting he said: First of all, this University is not going to close down. Yes some of the members of BOD and some ex-employees are in Police Custody and being interrogated. But all this is for the good of this

University. Our Chancellor too is cooperating in investigations. So I request all of you, students in particular, not to panic but concentrate on your studies. Yes, if any student or employee has any knowledge of any one involved in sale of fake certificates, he/she can give that information to me. I will relay this information to the Investigating agencies."

78

After six months of physical separation, day arrived when divorce of Prateeksha and Jitendra would be legalized in a Meerut Court. Prateeksha and her father Tejram reached in time. Jitendra, along with his father, Pardumman Singh, was 5 minutes late. As the couple stood before the Honorable Judge, time seemed to stand still for a while. Then the proceedings started.

"Do the 2 of you still want divorce?"

"Yes," said Prateeksha.

"What about you, Jitendra?"

"No."

Father and daughter both were surprised. It was Jitendra who pushed for divorce in first place. Judge raised his eyebrows.

"Me Lord, there were certain matters which got sorted out as late as yesterday. I misunderstood her in past, hence the acrimony between us. I apologize to her in your presence."

"What say, Prateeksha?' Judge asked the lady.

"Sir, can you give me 5 minutes for a private discussion?'

"Take 15 minutes, even more if you like and then return to the bench."

The four went into a huddle in a nearby park. "Papa I am sorry to have slighted you,' said Jitendra to his father-in-law, "but when I heard you are surrendering to law, I realized how unfair I had been to Prateeksha. Ever since Balbir tauji visited me and told me the whole story, I am full of remorse."

"Yes brother, forgive my son." Said Pardumman

"I am so happy Jitu. Fault was mine too. I wasn't prepared to listen anything against my father." Prateeksha wiped a tear drops from corner of her eyes.

Pardumman hugged her tight, "you did what any good daughter would do for her father. I am proud of you prati."

Bhaiyaji couldn't hold back his tears. Pardumman held his hand and consoled him. Sorrow is the fire that burns away our sins. He shouldn't worry about his family as long as Perdumman is alive.

The four presented themselves before the Judge after 20 minutes. Divorce proceedings were annulled.

79

"Hi papa, how are you?'

"Hi Veena, Reached Johannesburg safe?' Dev was excited hearing his daughter.

"Yes. But news from mummy is not good. Nanaji has been charge sheeted and his properties attached. Even Mom was called for questioning."

"Yes I know. But I can't help them. Your Nana has entangled himself in a web of his own making. Even you can't help them. Law has to take its course. We can only wait and watch."

"Papa there is one more Indian in our office apart from two of us. I couldn't meet her. Her name is Prateeksha and she is in Australia on an assignment."

"Name sounds familiar. Wonder where I heard it."

"She will be back next week, and then I will tell you more about her."

"How is Muskan, She must be completing one year now."

"Yes papa, she is healthy and playful. We leave her in crutch while coming to office. When she was born, she looked like me. Now she looks like Vipin."

"Ya, children change look. You too changed looks in your growing period."

"When are you coming to South Africa papa?'

"No plans as of now. But I will inform you in time."

"OK papa take care."

"Bye dear. God bless you."

As Dev turned back, he saw VC smiling.

"Good morning Sir."

"Good morning Dev. There is something important that I want to discuss with you. And by the way Prateeksha is our Chancellor's daughter. She is also serving in a multinational at Johannesburg."

"That's great. Sir there is a visitor in my office. I will spend 5 minutes with him and then come to your office."

Dev reached VC's office and found him sitting with Advocate Mr. Gurpal Saini, the new legal advisor of the University. In view of Bhaiyaji quitting Chancellor's post, a new Chancellor must be appointed to fill the gap. Who could be the next Chancellor of University was being discussed. Dev joined in with suggestion, "Sir you should move on to this post, and for VC we can float advertisement for a new incumbent."

"No Dr. Dev, all my relatives will blame me for chair snatching. I came here to help Tejram, not sit on his throne."

"Sir we need a person of impeccable integrity for this post, and that's not easy to find."

"I have found one and that's none other than Tejram's elder daughter Prateeksha, serving as senior manager in PWC South Africa. Presently she is in India and would be coming tomorrow to the University."

"Great! Good choice Sir."

"What a coincidence. I guess soul of late Ramjilal is uniting all good people in this University and that's a good omen. Please ask your daughter Veena also if she is willing to join as Executive Director in this University. We have already floated advertisement for it on our University web site."

"I will Sir."

80

Prateeksha was received by Brig. Sugriv Singh on the main gate. She touched his feet and asked him: "how are you mausaji?'

"Well beta. God bless you. We will head straight to the conference hall. People are waiting for you."

All stood up as the young lady escorted by VC entered the hall. "A very good morning to all of you, and please be seated," said VC. As house got seated, Brig. Sugriv said, "Ladies and gentleman, I have the honor to introduce to you our esteemed guest of day, Prateeksha Tomar."

Prateeksha got up and acknowledged the applause with folded hands. House too got up with her and continued clapping. In a while house was again seated. VC continued: "As most of you already know Prateeksha is going to be to be our next Chancellor and she will take charge in a month's time. She can't do it earlier because she has to fly back to Johannesburg, submit her resignation and get relieved from her present job. Without taking much of your time, I will now hand over the mike to Prateeksha."

"Thank you mausaji, and Honorable Vice Chancellor of this University," said Prateeksha getting up and accepting mike from Brig. Sugreev Singh, "Dean Admn. Dr. Dev, Deputy. Registrar Mr. Vikas, and all members of the teaching faculty. Normally if someone is suddenly elevated to a high post, it must be an occasion to rejoice. However I would sit on this chair in most unfortunate circumstances of my professional as well as personal life. My father and my brother-in-law have been charge sheeted in connection with fake degree racket which operated with active as well as passive support of many who served in this University at various positions. To err is human and our ex-chancellor, my father, is a human too. He trespassed on duty and will undergo punishment for same. My duty is to salvage name of my grand father Ramjilal on whose name this University is founded. In this gigantic task I will need cooperation of you all. Thank you all."

House once again clapped generously and thumped table. Prati covered her face with handkerchief. A fit of emotion choked her throat and tears trickled down her eyes. Trying frantically to gain her composure, she looked up and said, "I am sorry."

Brig. Sugreev again took to mike and said house was open to any kind of question either to him or to Madam Prateeksha.

81

Ancestral home of Col K. K. Verma in Baleni bore festive look. Col. was coming home after 40 years, along with wife Kamla, son Vikas, daughter- in- law Vinita and granddaughter Aashi. Vinita's parents too accompanied her.

Verma's younger brother Omprakash received him. Step brother Jaiprakash, and step sisters Daya and Ombati were also present. He hugged them all one by one. Then the family moved to the felicitation camp where entire village had gathered to honor Col. Verma.

Gram Pradhan Mahipal Singh gave key note address. Village Baleni is blessed in getting one of his illustrious sons back home. Some misunderstanding between him and his father Sohan Lal broke up Sohan family. Sans for Omprakash, Kailash bhai didn't have any dealing with his other brother and sisters. As a token repentance, he is transferring 5 acres of his land in name of his brother Jaiprakash and sisters Daya and Ombati. Transferring land into sister's names is not a norm in this area. It is a benchmark which Col. Kailash Kumar is setting. We are proud of him. He has also expressed desire to spend his last days in this village only.

Pradhan's address was widely cheered. Then Col KK was invited to dais. Col. said: "Thank you Pradhan Ji but I am neither setting any benchmark nor helping my extended family. I realize I was always a selfish man and even now I am looking to my own interest only. I always missed my village and smell of dung and animals. This village is my mother. I was born here and grew up to be an Army officer because of love and blessings of this soil. I can never pay back what I received from here. But I am trying to. Not only me but my son Vikas has also missed village. I am also returning Vikas to you. He is son of this village. Please love him and guide him like your own son."

Then it was the turn of Ompraksh to speak. He said his brother has always helped him. He has done his duty towards me, and now he is doing his bit for his other brother and sisters, and I am very happy about it. Two third of whatever is earned in the land donated by my brother, will be regularly conveyed to our sisters at their in-laws house; I will personally ensure this. I on behalf of this village and my own behalf, extend hearty invitation to my brother to spend rest of his life with us and enrich this village with his knowledge and experience. Jai Ram Ji Ki to all.

"And before the house disburses for tea and refreshment, I have one more announcement to make,' said Pradhanji taking mike from Omprakash, "Colonel Sahb has announced a grant of 1 lac for the village library and another 1 lac for organizing half marathon in this village every year. Marathon would be held on 1 july every year, that being the birthday of his late father Sohan Lal."

Very nice, very good, chanted all in audience. Some elderly ladies huddled with Vikas, and his mother Kamla. Vinita touched feet of elders guided by her mother on relationship she (Vinita) had with them. A lady from behind closed Vinita'a eyes: "guess who am I?' No idea, said Vinita. "I am your father's cousine sister Angoori, your bua. I recommended your marriage with Vikas.

At a distance Vinita's father Dr. Mukesh and mother kanti grinned from ear to ear, seeing their daughter subscribe to norm and decorum of village life.

"Take this,' said Angoori extending a 100 rupee note to Vinita.

"No buaji, please."

"Well this is not for you. It is for my granddaughter. What's her name?

"Aashi" said Vinita.

"Take it." Laughed Vikas. "Rs 100/- in these days of demonetization are an equivalent of a thousand rupees."

82

Dev's cell phone beeped at 2 a.m. at night. Who can it be? It was Veena.

"Yes Veena, why ring me at this odd time?'

"Papa I just wanted your advice on what to eat. For the last 20 hours I am working and taking only tea and snacks. Four hours of work is still left and I am feeling tired and hungry. What should I eat?'

"Don't eat, take only fruit juice. Retire for sleep immediately after finishing your work. Only on getting up from sleep should you take a square meal, that too after a cup of tea."

"Ok papa. And thanks for email. I have applied for the post of Executive Director in Ramjilal."

"Ok dear, can I sleep now?'

"Yes papa. Good night."

Dev slept till late in the morning. Attendant came to wake him up, as VC desired to see him. Dev got up hurriedly, took shower and headed straight to VC's office. VC welcomed him and asked about his health.

"I am fine sir. Just that slept late, so got up late."

"Dev I want to meet farmers from all adjoining villages. Organize a farmer's meet within a month's time. University is supposed to be a guiding light for people around. But I don't see anyone coming to University for any kind of guidance. This is surprising."

"I will get on job right now Sir."

Dev called for a safari jeep and drove out. He covered 10 villages and halted for an hour in each, talking to ladies, gents and any one he found willing to talk. The impression he gathered from them was that Ramjilal University belonged to a rich man and only the rich could study there. Some said atmosphere in University was not good. Student had gone on strike sometime back. Some said University sold fake degrees. To the query" have you visited University?" some said no, others said they never felt like, a few said they wanted to see University but security men stopped them at gate saying they must take prior permission of Registrar to see the campus.

Next day, Dev called Vikas and directed him to prepare a list of prominent farmers of 50 nearby villages. They would be invited to farmer's meet due to be organized in University next month.

83

CBI inspector Hema Ram was once again in University picking up threads of fake degree investigation. He wanted to know where abouts of Simmi Berwal, Dr. P C Yadav, Prof Naresh Mahajan and Dr. Badri Nath Tiwari so that he could approach them for their side of the story.

Vikas informed him that Mrs.Berwal, as per his personal knowledge, had gone abroad, probably to Canada. Her present address is not known to him. Why was she removed from the post of Dean Academics? Well, most likely because she failed to fulfill admission targets. She was appointed to knock off Prof. Mahajan who too had failed to meet admission targets.

"I heard that it was Simmi who brought in Dr. Tiwari as VC and Deepa Seth as his assistant in University. The three were colleagues in Manas Vidyapeeth. Then how come the then VC Dr.Tiwari recommend her sack?'

"He didn't sack her. In fact he was grateful to her for having got him appointed to VC's post. It was Bhaiyaji, our Chancellor who was miffed with her for not meeting even 10% admission targets. Initially Simmi too felt she has been ousted by Dr. Tiwari. She made scene in VC's office accusing Tiwari and Deepa of back stabbing her. It was with great difficulty that the two succeeded in convincing her that it was Bhaiyaji and not they who wanted her out."

"Where do I get her present address from?"

"From her personal file we can give you the address and phone number of her in-laws in Lucknow. You may contact them. As for the addresses of Dr. Yadav, Dr. Tiwari and Prof Mahajan, we will give you right now."

"Is it true that Dr. Tiwari and Miss Deepa were in relationship? Our sources say that for the past 10 years they served at 4 places and were together in all postings."

"Deepa is daughter of Dr. Tiwari's best friend. After her father's death he has treated her as his own daughter."

"Dr. Tiwari is married and has 3 children. He is estranged with his wife for the past 15 years."

"I have no knowledge of that. In University Dr. Tiwari lived alone."

"Was Dr. Tiwari engaged in some tantric rituals as well?"

"He used to perform Yagya or hawan and motivated teaching faculty for same. Once he called me to say that he knew of problems in my married life and that if I performed a particular Yagya, my problems would be over. I refused."

"Any other thing about Dr. Tiwari on this issue?'

"One day at about mid night I woke up to a commotion. As I opened the door a splash of water came on my face. Bhanu stood there with a bucket of water. He apologized profusely and said he intended to sprinkle water on the door and not me. He was directed to do so by Dr. Tiwari. Water was charged with some mantras and given to be sprinkled discreetly on the door of faculty apartments."

"That's interesting."

84

Prateeksha returned to her office in South Africa and gave one month's notice for resignation. She called Veena to her office; the two were meeting for the first time. Exigencies of duty kept them apart even as the two were in same office for the last 3 months.

"Nice meeting you Veena. I met your father, a thorough gentleman."

"Thanks madam."

"What madam? Call me didi, sister."

"Thanks didi."

"So, how is your family?'

"Well. My husband Vipin is Director here, presently in Italy for a project on Artificial Intelligence. We have a daughter, Muskan."

"I have heard a lot about Vipin. Lucky you. Got a great husband."

"Thanks didi."

"I am sure you have applied for the post of Executive Director in Ramjilal University."

"Yes."

"Then when are you resigning from here?"

"As and when I get appointed, I haven't even faced interview for that."

"As new Chancellor of this University it is in my hands who I select to this post. Your father says you are very hardworking. That's enough for me."

"Thanks, Didi. I understand your marriage is disturbed. I pray to God that your problems are solved as soon as possible."

"It's solved already. My husband has patched up with me. We are one again."

"That's great Didi."

"Yes, that indeed is good news. Apart from this, there is no good news on my side."

“Father gave me some hint about it. But you don’t worry. Time is a great healer.”

“Thanks, Veena. Let’s come to the point. I will be relieved from here in a month’s time. In a week’s time you also tender your resignation. You will get your appointment letter on the day you visit University.”

85

Farmer's meeting was chaired by VC, Brig. Sugriv Singh. In his key-note address he said University is a pool of knowledge for the society. But unfortunately, I see no one in the surrounding villages taking advantage of this knowledge pool. No farmer ever comes to the Department of Agriculture and Life Sciences. We have a legal cell which can help farmers with legal matters. Our PR section can take farmer's grievances to concerned departments and even to media. We have a gym and a swimming pool which can be used by the public. But these resources are not being used, why?

"You are telling us for the first time."

"Yes, and we regret that. We should have told you long back, but as they say, better late than never."

"Do you have some department for Animal Husbandry also? We don't have a Veterinary hospital nearby."

"Yes, our Dean Administration Dr. Dev is a Veterinary Doctor. Another Doctor, Dr. Mukesh is looking after our in-campus dairy farm and teaching Animal Husbandry to B.Sc. Agriculture students. You can avail their services anytime. Dr. Dev is a Poultry Expert. And Dr. Mukesh is an expert in treatment of large animals."

"We heard a lot about sale of fake documents from this University. Your Chancellor is in jail for that. How can people have faith in such University?

"Our Chancellor had voluntarily surrendered to State Administration. He has confessed to his wrong doings and agreed to help CBI in stemming out rot in Higher education. This is a new beginning and should be welcomed by one and all."

"Can your experts visit our village time to time and solve our problems at our door steps. We will pay them for their service."

"We can start this service right from tomorrow. An Advocate, a Veterinary Doctor and an Agriculture expert will visit nodal villages once in a week. Those desirous of taking their services can collect in those villages. For six months fee charged will be in the form of donation. This donation will be ploughed back into our rural services. In time we can work out a fee package for different   services."

Meeting touched upon many areas of rural development and youth welfare. It was also decided to open a `Carriers and Competition' cell in University where students from nearby villages could be groomed for competitive examinations. University playground could be used by villagers to organize events and carnivals. Any farmer can walk into University campus without prior appointment.

At the end of the meeting house dispersed for lunch. After lunch farmers were taken for a guided tour of the University campus.

86

Master Jagdish was charged by the economic offence wing for possessing assets disproportionate to his known sources of income. He had borrowed 20 lakhs to get his son admitted to medical college through donation. Hearing of vigilance raid on him, creditors started pressing for their money. He was forced to pay up by way of assigning his LIC policies, Jewelry and Savings certificates. Creditors were mafia and carried loaded revolver in their pocket. Stripped to bone and doing countless rounds of investigating agency, Jagdish slipped into mental depression. With a married and jobless son at home and another in medical college, his salary as teacher was drop in ocean.

That day as he returned from School on scooter, he was hit from behind. Tossed high up, he fell to instant death. Whether it was accident or murder, could never be ascertained. His wife maintained that a relative owed them some 50 lakhs but refused to pay it. No evidence could be produced as it was black money. That relative, she maintained, contrived to eliminate her husband. Whatever, Jagdish family was literally on road.

Veena informed her father about the tragedy. Dev rushed to Delhi and paid his last respect to his father-in-law. Dead body seemed diminutive and light. Some expressed fear that his organs may have been removed in Hospital where the dead body was kept in cold room for identification.

Jagdish was son of poor farmer and financed his own education through tuitions, loans and part time jobs. Somewhere down the line he went astray, goaded by his wife to earn-more for the marriage of their two daughters and settlement of their two sons. Parents strive to ease their children's life forgetting that the life of their children is not a continuum of the life which they themselves have lived. Each Life is a different story, set in a different time frame.

87

"Any question on Breeding Practices in cows and buffaloes?' Asked Dr. Mukesh Prajapati.

One student got up, "is one mating or one artificial insemination (AI), enough for conception?'

"It may or may not be. If animal doesn't conceive in one attempt, go for second chance in next heat, even 3rd if animal again comes in heat after 21 days. If animal comes in heat for 4th time, then you can rate animal as repeat breeder and consult Doctor for a possible disease or a management fault."

"Sir AI must surely deprive a dam of sexual pleasure which she may get with bull mount in natural service. Don't you think this impacts rate of conception?"

"Please don't confuse sexual activity of an animal with that of a human being. Animals don't fantasize as humans do. Animals just react to their hormonal surges. They are not pleasure seekers like men."

"But sir sex is central to existence and propagation of all life forms. AI seems to have deprived sex of its glamour and natural attraction."

"Wife of a retired army officer asked me same question and I couldn't convince her that AI was more effective tool for reproduction than natural service. But here in classroom environment I think I should be able to explain. Let me begin by quoting a philosopher: to drink when not thirsty, and to make love in all seasons, madam, that's all the difference between man and animal. See the love and attraction we attach to sex is more matter of perception than reality. A man dying of hunger will ask for food and water, not sex. We enjoy eating, drinking, talking and frolicking; sex is just another item to this list with caveats. Caveat is that sex is a luxury function and not an essential or lifesaving activity. First there is the question of food and safety, then and then only sex comes in picture. In humans' sex has been commercialized to such a great extent that we grow up believing it is the best that life has to offer. But this is not true. In itself sex is an act of skin rub. It's going upscale many folds is all thanks to man's tremendous ability to dream and visualize."

"I agree with you sir,' said one married student, "anticipation is sweeter than realization."

There was laughter in class. Another student got up to say that ideally marriage is for a social obligation to carry one's lineage forward, not for sex.

"I am impressed by your statement,' said Dr. Mukesh," but you are too young to really profess this lofty ideology."

"This is what my grandfather professed. I only borrowed from his conviction."

"Interesting."

"My grandfather was a famed wrestler in his youth. He is 95 years and still active in agriculture and animal husbandry."

"Great. Tell us more about him."

"My grandfather has 4 sons. And he tells us with pride that he got physical with our grandmother only four times in his life. Each time they met, conception happened."

"But sir you said conception may not be there with one mating."

Class was again in splits. Dr. Mukesh advised returning to main topic. Human reproduction would be taken up some other time.

"So, as I said, animals follow hormonal changes in their body. When AI is successful, and pregnancy begins, urge for sex is switched off by another hormone. Since animals are not imaginative, they scarce think how they conceived. In fact many a dams refuse bull mount as that is a traumatic experience for them. But AI is a gentle procedure and they accept it without fuss. Some animal care groups view AI as cruelty. But I disagree with them. Their perception is flawed because they try to apply idea of human mating to the idea of animal mating. Natural service may at times be cruel, but Artificial Insemination is never cruel."

"AI is becoming popular in humans as well, as shown in film Vicky donor."

"Right."

88

Prateeksha joined as Chancellor of Ramjilal University. That same day she addressed press conference. She gave vision statement of the University and introduced her staff to the media. Then she declared floor open for questions.

"Madam your father and brother-in-law are in Jail. Admissions are going down year by year. Many Private Universities have already closed down for lack of admissions. How do you think you will be able to survive under these circumstances?'

"I have a team of dedicated professionals. We will do our best and I am sure we will achieve much more than a mere survival."

"Your brother-in-law has siphoned money to foreign bank accounts and it is alleged that you and your sister actively helped him in doing that?"

"Rubish. Infact I and my sister revealed those accounts to investigating agencies."

"You and your sister have been paid a hefty salary of 80,000 per month by the University even as you served in other companies and never took any class...."

"This was done by our father without our knowledge. We have taken cognizance of this amount and this amount would be recovered from my father's assets."

"Upright teachers and administrators have been sacked from this University and their careers ruined. What about them?"

"I have constituted a board to go through their personal files. Files did reveal inconsistencies. We have written to them that their cases are being reopened and if any injustice is found done to them, they would be suitably compensated."

"Many students were admitted in this University for courses which were not available in University. After admitting them they were forced to opt for available courses. Those who didn't accept switch lost academic year and their fee deposit. Their fee was not returned."

"We have compiled a list of such students and we are in the process of refunding all their dues."

"Regulatory bodies have given a very poor report about this University."

"I have seen that report. But let me tell you that Regulatory bodies themselves are under scanner. Their relevance and way of working is being seriously questioned. If regulatory bodies did their job sincerely, higher education wouldn't be in the mess we find it today."

"In pharmacy a total of 60 students are shown roll. But only 2 students attend classes regularly."

"I must complement you for digging out this information. I have called explanation of Dr. Murlidhar. I will get his response within a week. Then I will be able to say something on this issue."

"A lady came to us saying she was appointed in Ramjilal and then removed by University just after 7 days. She said she was removed because she refused to sleep with registrar Col. Jagdeep."

"Col Jagdeep is no more in University. If the lady feels her case is strong, she can sue Col. Jagdeep, we can help her by providing her access to Col. Jadeep's personal file which is kept in our record."

"Students of your University were caught selling drugs. Some were also involved in theft of a car."

"Yes. And we extended all cooperation to the police department in nabbing them. But please don't tell me we were teaching them to sell drugs and steal vehicles."

"But it reflects the kind of discipline that prevails in campus."

"We are going for a total revamp in all departments of University. And soon you will find a change in overall discipline of University. All we need is your cooperation. Please feel free to walk into campus any time you feel like and give us your feedback. As for advertisements, I assure you all that presently we are cash strapped and have no money for advertisement. I need a minimum of 1 year time to set things right."

Conference concluded with a note of thanks by Dr. Dev Purohit.

89

Post demise of Jagdish, the school teacher, there were speculations whether Parul, his daughter, would go back to her in-laws. Seniors prevailed she should. Dev too was advised that he should rethink and bring her back.

Dev said Parul left on her own, he never asked her to leave. In fact he went to her repeatedly requesting her to return as her rightful place was with him, not with her parents. He was not in a position to buy her a new house, so she should live with his parents. Half the cost of house at Meerut was borne by Dev. So, house belonged as much to Dev, as to his parents. But Parul wouldn't live with Dev's parents and sister.

"Why don't you divorce her if she is so adamant?" Some relatives suggested.

"For two reasons, one I have no intention to remarry. Two, I want to prove in my life time how cruel a woman can be. She can ruin her husband's life and still pass as innocent victim of male chauvinism."

"But you are doing well in your career. Your daughter is well settled in her career and married in a nice family."

"Simply because I didn't commit suicide or go mad, people believe all is well. As for my daughter, she is married to the boy she loved. My otherwise disastrous marriage has given me caring daughter and a loving son-in-law. I am immensely grateful to God for this blessing."

"Still you must show magnanimity and bring her home."

"To increase my problems all the more; is that what you want?"

"Ok, you put your conditions and we will convey them to her. May be she agrees."

"My condition is that she should apologize for spreading rumor that I suffer from AIDs that's why she doesn't live with me. She should also apologize for spreading canard that I forced her to sleep with another man. If she does that, I will bring her home."

"That's very unbecoming of her, if what you say is true."

"She wanted a strong reason to remain away from me and hide that she is a fake graduate. So she invented a slew of incredible stories to paint me as man of loose character. She and her family should also apologize for fixing my marriage to her on the basis of fake educational qualifications."

90

Dev reached Delhi Airport to receive Veena at 4 a.m. in the morning. By 8 a.m. they reached Ramjilal University. Veena would report in University at 10 a.m. and meet Prateeksha, the new Chancellor.

"Papa, can I keep mom with me here in University? Vipin will continue his job in Johannesburg. Muskan will live with me. I want mother to take care of Muskan," said Veena, unwinding in her father's apartment

"Ask Vipin."

"I have asked him, he is okay with it."

"Ask your mother also whether she agrees for it. You know she never agrees to what I say."

"Yes," laughed Veena, "in fact the condition she has put is that you shouldn't be living under same roof."

"Thank God she didn't say in-the- same-campus."

Father and Daughter had a hearty laugh. By 10 a.m. they were in Chancellor's office.

"Good morning Dr. Dev. Welcome Veena," said Chancellor.

"Good morning madam."

"Veena here is your appointment letter. Read it well. Take rest for today and you can join duty tomorrow. Have a nice day."

"Take keys of my apartment." Said Dev as Veena got up to leave.

There was a file before Prati and she was furiously perusing it.

"Madam may I help you with file work?"

"Yes Dev. I am confused about the PF issues. There is a letter from PF department penalizing us for defaulting on PF payment. Please go through these files and give me exact picture of where we stand."

"Yes madam. Give me a day."

91

Dev took file to his office and called Vikas for assistance.

University had argued with PF commissioner that a private University was under no obligation to give PF to its employees. In support of this argument a past case of a private company not subscribing to PF was cited. Company was sued by the PF Commissioner. Supreme Court finally ruled in favor of Company. If that company could enjoy exemption to PF, why not Ramjilal University?

PF commissioner rebutted argument saying the case cited was different. The Company in question did have an effective savings scheme in place for her employees; hence PF was waived for them. But Ramjilal has no saving scheme whatsoever for her employees. Therefore the University doesn't deserve waiver of PF scheme. He also refused to believe that teaching faculty was being paid such low salaries as shown in salary sheet.

Many correspondences later a bunch of affidavits were presented to Commissioner. These were from teaching staff, each saying he/she joined University at low salary on his/her own volition and that he/she was not compelled to accept low wages. Affidavit further said the signatory joined University with missionary zeal to use his knowledge for the service of society.

PF Commissioner laughed at the lame excuse University gave and imposed a fine of 2 lakhs. He further directed University to ensure deduction of PF of all employees with immediate effect. University's PF case was being handled by the ex-legal advisor Vinesh Sharma. Dev explained case to Chancellor Madam and suggested file be handed over to new legal advisor for necessary action.

"No. Don't do that," said Prateeksha, "Pay the fine asked for and deduct PF for all employees beginning this month. Then give me a comparative account of what our teaching staff is actually being paid as against scales recommended by regulatory bodies."

"OK Madam."

92

"What? Brig. Sugriv has resigned?'

Word spread like wild fire. Students rushed to his office. After such a long time University was coming on rails. How can VC leave them at this crucial stage? VC requested them to collect in lawn where he would address the gathering.

Brig took to mike. After ceremonial address to Chancellor, office bearers and students he said he came to University with a purpose. The purpose has been achieved and there is nothing more left for him to do in the University. He is a man of administration and finished his job of reviving and fine tuning the administration of the University. Now a new VC was required who should be an academician. He is giving way for such incumbent who would take University to new heights. He expressed satisfaction that University was now in the hands of young blood like Prateeksha and Veena. Able guardians like Dr. Dev, Dr. Mukesh and Vikas Verma will see to it that University rises to a level of Global University in real sense of the term. Please do not come in my way as I am an emotional person and may get carried away. I have done my bit for University and must now move on. There are other people who look to me for help and company. I have been selected as Secretary to the league of retired Army men. Now I want to work for my professional colleagues who served this nation in the prime of their life time but are facing problem in their retirement. Hope you will allow me to work for them. Thank you for your love and cooperation in this campus.

As he finished, there was stunning silence for a moment. Dr. Dev woke up to clap. Others too followed. Clapping continued for long till VC raised his hand for silence. Sensing gloom in audience, Brigadier tried to cheer them: "now I will give you a good news." Everyone looked up.

"First cheer up and smile, then I will reveal it. Yes, that's it. Now listen, Dr. Naresh Mahajan is coming back to University."

There was spontaneous applause from students and teachers both.

"And he isn't coming as Pro VC that he was in his earlier assignment with the University. He is coming back as Vice Chancellor. He will be here in a week's time and then I will leave."

93

"Uncle Do you believe in destiny? Question came from Vinita. This was her way of starting a conversation in family. Dr. Dev responded, "Yes, I think I do."

"But Papa says you don't."

"That was when I was in college."

"What? You always explained to me how we always get in life what we really want." Dr. Mukesh chipped in.

"My opinion is same even now. But my vision has grown many folds."

"And your vision says destiny is everything. And what of hard work, dedication, determination, etc you lived and swore by?"

"They are everything. But who knows that you were destined to succeed by way of hard work and not without hard work?"

"Wow uncle, what an answer!"

"Vinita life is a constant challenge. Challenges never end. Buddhism explains it best. It says you can never step into same waters twice. Try doing it. Your second step in water is received by a different body of water. Similarly environment around us is constantly changing. We can never really say we have adjusted to our environment, because our environment is changing every second. We ourselves too, are changing every second."

"Yes Vinita. Dev is right. Do you know the definition of good health?"

"Good health is when all our body functions are within the range of normal, as prescribed by Medical Science," said Vinita.

"No, many people with normal parameters feel ill at ease. Good health is not so easy to attain. Ideally health is a state in which an individual is correctly adjusted to all irritants of existence."

"Right Dr. Mukesh," Observed Dev, "since environment and individual both are constantly changing, good health is a never-ending challenge."

"Uncle let's return to destiny. Now tell me, is it destiny that you and Aunty remain separate or it is lack of efforts on your part to patch up."

"I guess it was both, destiny as well as lack of efforts. She grew up as traditionalist. I grew up as an antagonist, pining for revolution. Environment which clubbed us together was somewhere in between. It was neither traditionalist nor revolutionary. We couldn't adjust to this environment. I held to my own ways of raw eating and natural ways. She held on to her own traditional ways. So our parting had to happen. We made efforts to pull on with each other for full 14 years. That's quite an achievement."

"Good analysis uncle."

"And what do you say about Bhaiyaji of Ramjilal University?

"Well that again is destiny, like that of my father-in-law Jagdish. Both Tejram and Jagdish had a painful childhood of poverty and deprivation. When destiny smiled on them, they should have become fearless about future. But unfortunately, the more they earned, the more fearful they became about their future, about their children's future. That did them in."

"What about those who bought fake degrees and ruined their careers?"

"They were chasing a dream. Half of our life is spent in sleeping, and that means dreaming. Add to this the number of movies we see, fiction we read and the day dreaming we do. Then what you have is more of dreams and very less of realistic down to earth living. And what are fake documents if not dream? We die in our dreams many times before real death comes knocking."

"What's the solution then?"

"Do dream but do daring as well. Love adversities, hardships. Not in a way of inviting them by stupid acts but in the manner of accepting positive challenges. Hard work will keep your dreams rooted to reality."

"But we are so afraid of hardships that we pray to God for happiness and prosperity."

"Not all. Kunti, the mother of Pandavas prayed for boon of adversity. To flabbergasted Krishna, she explained that the adversities made her remember Krishna and that kept her in bliss. This episode from Mahabharata is metaphoric. It turns the prevailing concept of pain and pleasure, success and failure, on its head. Life is a continuum of challenges. Those who seek amnesty from challenges, find pain. Those who accept challenges, find liberation, salvation, supreme bliss. So, let's pray to God: give us this day, our daily task."

Dinner was laid out on table. Menu was a generous mug of fruit juice, baked potatoes and salad.

*****